A FATAL AUTUMNAL STEW

DAHLIA DONOVAN

HOT TREE PUBLISHING

ALSO BY DAHLIA DONOVAN

The Skeleton Crew Paranormal Cozy Series

A Curse For Samhain | A Fatal Autumnal Stew | A Merry Murderous Midwinter

The Grasmere Cottage Mystery Trilogy

Dead in the Garden | Dead in the Pond | Dead in the Shop

Motts Cold Case Mystery Series

Poisoned Primrose | Pierced Peony | Pickled Petunia | Purloined Poinsettia

London Podcast Mystery Series

Cosplay Killer | Ghost Light Killer | Crown Court Killer

Honey Bear Cosy Mysteries

Honey Mead Murder | Honey Bee Murder | Honey Moon Murder

Stand-alone Romances

After the Scrum | At War With A Broken Heart | Forged in Flood | Found You | By the Fire | One Last Heist | Pure Dumb Luck | Here Comes The Son | All Lathered Up | Not Even A Mouse | Farm to Fabre | The Misguided Confession | Stubbed Toes & Dating Woes

For information, contact the publisher, Tangled Tree Publishing.

WWW.HOTTREEPUBLISHING.COM

EDITING: Hot Tree Editing

COVER DESIGNER: BookSmith Design

MAP DESIGN: The Illustrated Page Book Design

E-BOOK ISBN: 978-1-923252-12-7

PAPERBACK ISBN: 978-1-923252-13-4

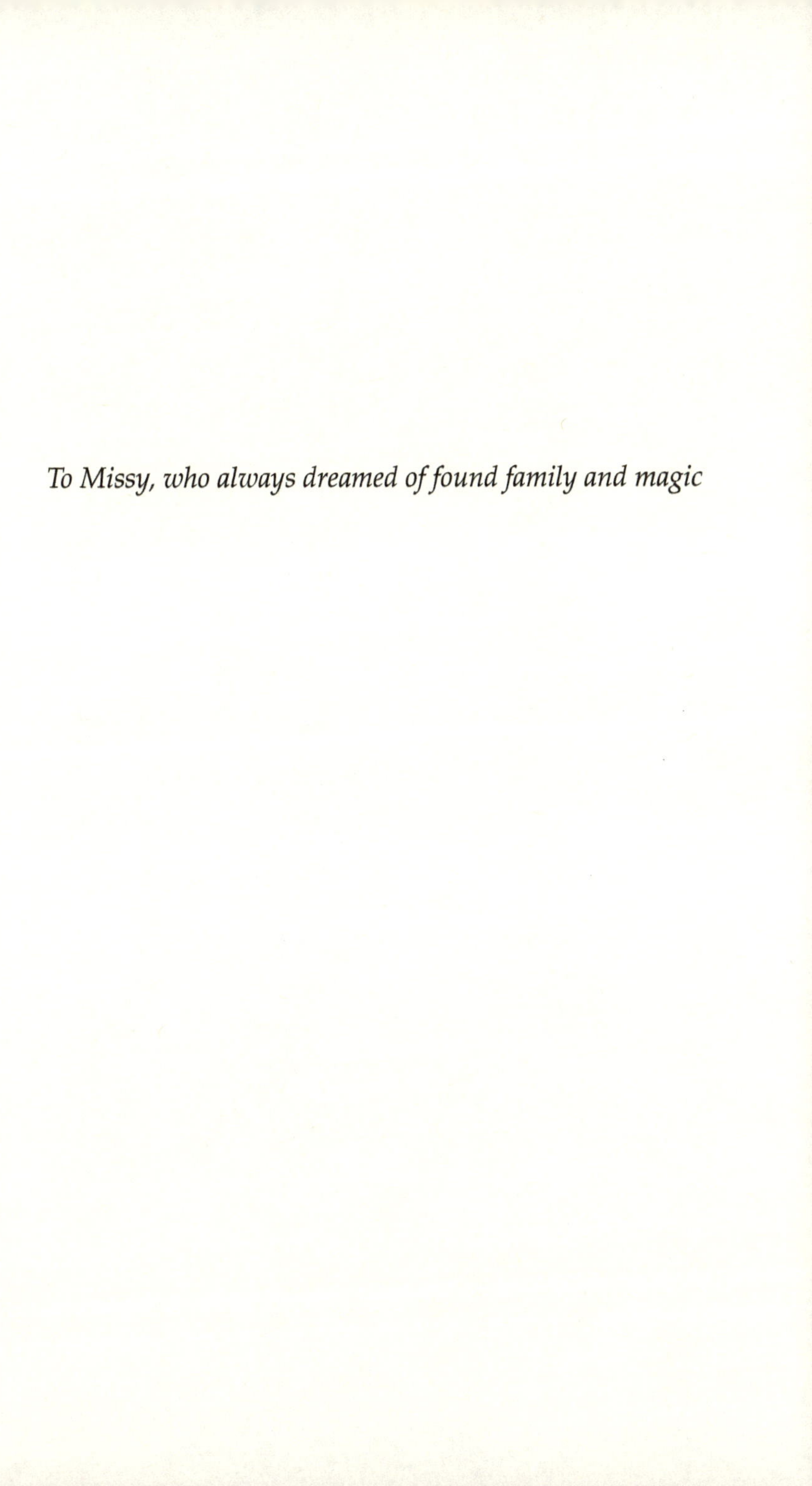

To Missy, who always dreamed of found family and magic

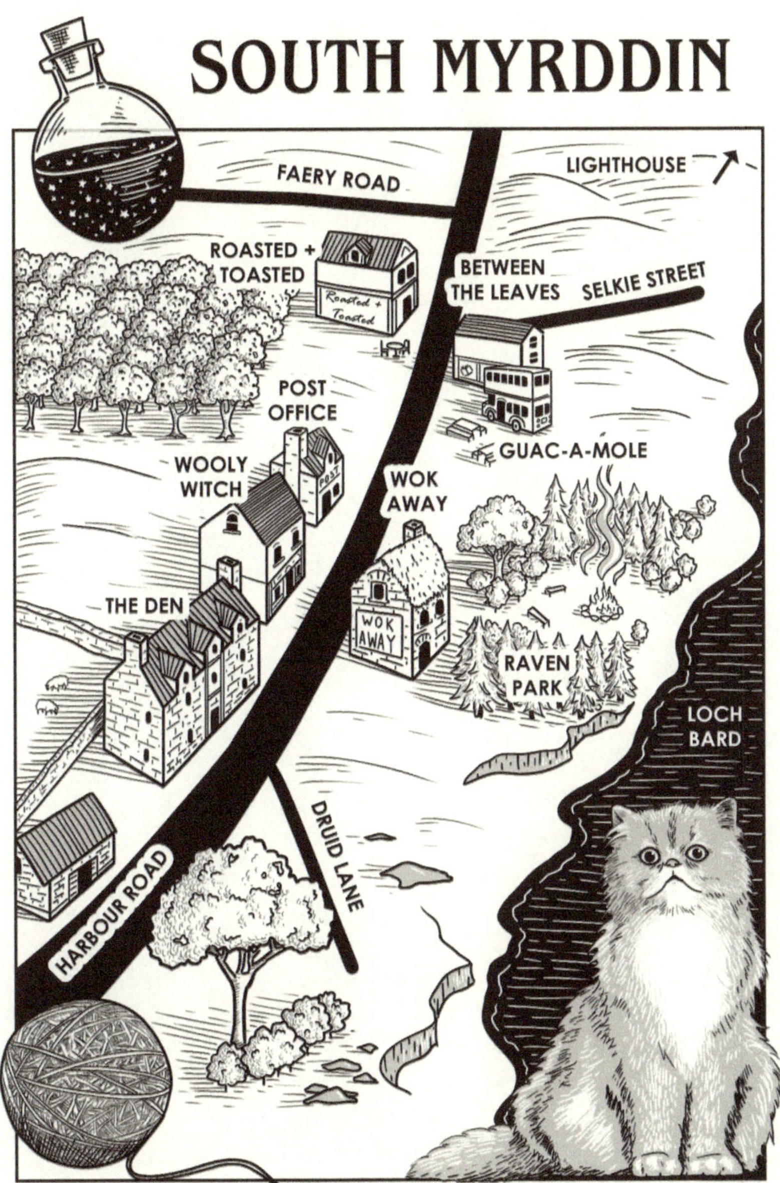

SOUTH MYRDDIN
FAERY ROAD
LIGHTHOUSE
ROASTED + TOASTED
Roasted + Toasted
BETWEEN THE LEAVES
SELKIE STREET
POST OFFICE
POST
WOOLY WITCH
WOK AWAY
GUAC-A-MOLE
WOK AWAY
THE DEN
RAVEN PARK
LOCH BARD
HARBOUR ROAD
DRUID LANE

1

HYDE

"Do not deface the cover." Hyde narrowed their eyes at the ginger fluffy marshmallow of a cat. Pestle stretched a paw out and set it on the book. "I'll give Mortar your last baked treat."

Bright yellow eyes glowered at them for the briefest second before he finally flounced over to the fireplace in the bookshop. Mortar, the more sedate of the two cats, a beautiful Persian with stunning blue eyes, barely acknowledged his presence. They both settled down on the mound of blankets for a nap.

"You are adorable menaces, and I love you." Hyde gave both of them the lightest of touches before going over to rescue the book in question. They grabbed the bottle of blood on the counter and sipped the last of it. "Battista might try roasting both

of you over a slow fire after all the work I did to find this for him and Amalia."

Amalia Bassani and Battista Sartor were a succubus and incubus who ran the local Creole-Italian restaurant. Al Dente was one of Hyde's favourite places to eat. The two had asked them to hunt for an ancient Roman scroll on their species.

Hyde Snodgrass, a vampire, autistic, and chubby ginger icon, was the proud owner of Between the Leaves, the lone bookshop in South Myrddin, a small village in the Scottish Highlands. They specialised in many things, including hunting down rare books.

The village had been their home since they were a small fanged child. South Myrddin was the home of the foundling. Abandoned magical people of all varieties found their way to the one place guaranteed to welcome them. It was why it had been founded in the first place.

Picking up the manuscript, Hyde wrapped it delicately in a paper that Battista had given them for protection. The book was old, though not as old as the original. They thought, however, it was a true translation of what had probably been a scroll as opposed to a bound book.

From their extensive research, nothing had been lost in translation. Hyde hoped their incubus and succubus friends found the answers they were looking for. The two had been tight-lipped about what they wanted to discover.

Hyde didn't mind. For them, the excitement of hunting down rare books was more than enough satisfaction. They glanced first at the clock on the wall and then at the bookshelves. "Time for a quick dust before I close up."

For most of the cleaning in the shop, Hyde relied on the three brownies who ran Feather Duster, the village cleaners. Dusting was the one job they did themselves, as they didn't want to risk any damage to some of the older books. Cleaning products tended to make their nose burn and their skin itch, so they had gratefully handed off those duties to the Lyalls.

Between the Leaves was the quintessential quaint village bookshop with a few differences. One section at the back was set up with a selection of armchairs around a coffee table. It was where their weekly knitting and crocheting group, the Skeleton Crew, met at least once a week.

Hyde grabbed the duster and began to go across the shelves lightly. They deftly avoided the burgundy lights twinkling above each shelf—a bit of magic gifted to them by Morrigan, who ran the village post office.

Moving to the front of the shop, Hyde went over the edges of the doorframe. They dusted the counter briefly and made sure the two signs were correct. It helped their life go more smoothly.

The first sign signified whether the day was a quiet one or not. The Shh spelt things out nicely for everyone. Sometimes, Hyde just couldn't put together sentences.

Their second sign had They on one side and She on the other. Some days, Hyde felt more one or the other. The village was always good about paying attention and respecting their wishes.

It took no time at all for Hyde to finish dusting. They were, in reality, putting off preparing for the evening. And they didn't want to be late for the date with Teresa.

Teresa Vega was a witch and the proud owner of the taco truck parked in front of the bookshop. Guac-A-Mole served a variety of tacos in mole sauce. They were all family recipes from the Mexican coven that her father had been a part of. Her grandmother had been the one to gift her with them after she'd been exiled.

The two had begun dating a few weeks earlier amidst the debacle of trying to find the person who'd killed one of the local village crones—Florence Batch. Teresa was everything Hyde felt they weren't. She had a cool and edgy vibe with her various tattoos and vintage motorcycle.

Peering out through the autumnal-themed stained-glass window of the front door, Hyde spotted Teresa closing up the taco truck. Guac-A-Mole took up the first level of a vintage double-decker bus while she lived on the second floor. She'd put a lot of work into the renovations of her business.

Hyde tapped on the window to get Teresa's attention. She spun around with a wide grin and held up both hands to signal ten minutes. "All right, Mortar and Pestle. Let's get you situated upstairs. No sneaking out of the bookshop."

The cats had managed to figure out how to open most of the doors in the shop and flat above it. Hyde trusted them not to get themselves into too much danger. They were clever creatures who behaved most of the time.

"Not on the jumper." Hyde sighed when Mortar immediately leapt onto the bed and curled up on the burgundy-coloured sweater. "I planned on wearing that this evening."

Since the silvery-grey beast claimed it, Hyde went to the wardrobe to find another. They went for a wheat-coloured one instead, pairing it with a deep brown blazer and their favourite corduroy trousers. There was barely enough time to dart into the en suite for the quickest of showers and get dressed before Teresa rang the bell downstairs.

It made a soft and cheery chime. Emrys had fixed the old one that had been so shrill that Hyde had covered their ears every time it went off. The old druid had done a lot around the bookshop to make them comfortable. He tended to take the foundlings of the village under his wing.

According to gossip and folklore, Emrys was the oldest resident. Some wondered if he'd been the Myrddin of legend who'd founded the village. He was dedicated to the abandoned magical beings who made their way to the one place that accepted them regardless of their oddities or differences.

South Myrddin was a warm embrace in an oft-cold world. They weren't perfect, but everyone found their way in the little village by the loch. It always welcomed them.

Putting thoughts of the village and Emrys out of their mind, Hyde dragged their fingers through their mess of ginger curls before shoving a blue flat cap over it. It didn't surprise them at all to find Teresa looking as devilishly attractive and suave as ever. Dark jeans, a Wayward Hags concert T-shirt, a leather jacket, long brown hair perfectly imperfect. The tattoos on her hands were the only ones visible.

"Hello." Teresa's smile widened. She stepped over and reached up to adjust Hyde's cap before leaning in for a kiss. "Ready for an Italian feast?"

"I... yes," Hyde stammered. They held up the carefully wrapped book. "And I've got their book."

"Excellent. Amalia promised to make her stracotto alla fiorentina. I love a good pot roast, and theirs is always beautifully tender. It's the perfect autumnal stew." Teresa brushed her hand against Hyde's before interlacing their fingers. "How was your day?"

Hyde shrugged. They never enjoyed small talk, even from Teresa. "Day-like."

"How about I ask a better question?" Teresa leaned into them a little. Her smile was genuine and sweet, with no sign of mocking in her tone. "Did the furred menaces enjoy the treat I sent over for breakfast?"

Hyde smiled at their girlfriend. "They did."

Girlfriend. We're dating. We've had a date. Dates, even. Is she my girlfriend?

"Are you my girlfriend?" Hyde blurted the question, then closed their eyes and groaned. "I didn't mean to say that out loud."

"I am. I'm sure some people would think it far too fast to claim titles of any sort in our relationship, but sod them. We've known each other for years. I figure we've slowly been dating without admitting it for much of that time." Teresa rubbed her thumb across Hyde's hand soothingly. "And you're my chubby ginger bookshop owner who I adore to pieces."

"Not literally. I like my pieces put together." Hyde loved the almost musical lilt to Teresa's laugh.

They were brought up short when a loud caw overhead signalled the arrival of Odin, who perched on their shoulder. He pecked Hyde's neck gently and pointed his beak towards the post office across the street. "Okay. Okay. Mind the skin."

"We appear to have been summoned." Teresa reached up to lightly tease Odin's tail feather, dodging away from his beak. "You don't get to peck my Hyde without some sort of retaliation."

My Hyde.

Hyde's brain stuttered over the words. *My Hyde. She's definitely my girlfriend. Definitely.*

Witch and witch's familiar poked and pecked each other all the way to the post office. Hyde ignored them, focused instead on discovering why Odin had left Morrigan. He was something of a seeing-eye bird to his blind companion.

"Hello, little duck."

Hyde rolled their eyes at Rees Mohan, a werewolf who owned the village fish and chip shop, the Malt Moon. "Is Morrigan all right? We were summoned by the feathered god of war."

"I am fine. They are overdramatic and paranoid."

Morrigan whistled softly from the post office door-way, causing Odin to fly from Hyde's shoulder to hers. He guided her over to where they were standing just outside it. "I'm sure it's nothing."

"And I think it's something. So does Santi," Rees snapped. He sighed and pinched the bridge of his nose. His eyes slowly returned to dark brown from slightly glowing hazel. "I'm sorry. I'm concerned."

"Maybe you could tell us what's happening? I'm confused." Hyde tried not to laugh at how Odin kept gently tugging Morrigan's black hair. It was soft, shiny, and wavy. It always reminded them of the way ink flowed out of a bottle. "Are you hurt?"

"I'm fine." Morrigan turned slightly toward Odin, who butted his head against hers, then tugged on her hair once again. She led them all inside the post office, stepping behind the counter. "I am. I promise."

"Well, that's really cleared things up." Teresa glanced at Hyde, who shrugged. They both turned to Rees, who'd joined them at the counter.

"There have been some oddities with mail. It arrives with no return address." Rees gestured to a heavy metal box on the end of the counter. "And once Morrigan touches the envelope, it explodes."

"Explodes?" Teresa reached out to grasp Morrig-an's hands. She carefully inspected them. "You said you weren't hurt."

"I know how to handle curses. And it's not an actual explosion—more of a magical release. I can't determine if it's tied to me directly or some form of timed spell. I've never seen the like." Morrigan shifted uneasily, pulling her hands away from Teresa. "I haven't mentioned it to the coven because I don't have anything to show. The remnants of the spell vanish. Rees can't smell or feel anything. They don't seem to do any harm."

"I could—"

"You are not licking cursed letters." Teresa firmly shut down what she had correctly assumed was Hyde's thought.

When Teresa's taco truck had been broken into, Hyde's hypersensitivity had come in handy for once. They'd been able to help identify a particular metal used. Their vampire senses were already elevated; being autistic only exacerbated the situation.

"Have you talked to Emrys or one of the druids? How would someone even manage a time-controlled curse in an envelope?" Teresa had moved on from thinking about licking to inspect the contents of the metal box where the evidence was stored. "Have you called the police yet?"

"You two should head to Al Dente." Rees nodded towards the door. "Santi went to get Emrys since he wasn't answering his phone. I'll make sure we call the police as well."

"Maybe Fynn. He might be best equipped," Hyde suggested. They were hesitant to leave such an intriguing mystery.

"I've got it." Morrigan slapped her hand against the counter, causing Hyde to jump in surprise. Odin cawed at his witch. "Sorry, ducky, I didn't mean to startle you."

"What have you got?" Teresa placed a calming hand on Hyde's arm.

"An idea about the letters. Now off you pop. The dinner at Al Dente sounds like it will be filled with drama. Amalia seems to have invited half of her family." Morrigan shooed them towards the door. "I promise to let you know if we discover anything."

"Which half of her family?" Rees asked as they were leaving.

"The half that she hates."

2

TERESA

"Why would Amalia invite the family who exiled her?" Hyde clutched the manuscript under one arm while Teresa held their other hand. They were halfway to Al Dente when they'd broken the silence. "To a celebration?"

"Maybe she wants to rub the manuscript in their faces."

"I am aware, logically, that you're not being literal. The idea of rubbing a precious manuscript in someone's face hurts my soul." Hyde smiled, a rare wide one that offered a flash of fang. "I am now imagining rubbing an old law book in Chief Inspector Pacheco's face—and it is a glorious vision."

Choking on a laugh, Teresa had to grasp Hyde's hand more tightly for support. It was easy to imagine the response from the stern man, who happened to be the highest-ranking vampire in the area coven. He also tended to annoy just about everyone in the village.

Chief Inspector Pacheco was a traditionalist when it came to magical families and covens. He might mean well, but he didn't always understand the nature of foundlings and South Myrddin. Hyde butted heads with him quite frequently.

"If I promise to make your favourite mole de moronga tacos, will you do it the next time you see him? Please?" Teresa couldn't stop snickering at the visual of the staid vampire having a book rubbed in his face. "I even have a new recipe to try."

While hunting through the various recipes in her family grimoire, Teresa had stumbled onto a new one for moronga—a type of blood sausage akin to chorizo. She'd had to order a few of the spices, but the local farm had provided the other ingredients. It was always good to have Hyde taste-test the vampire- and shifter-friendly menu items.

And they spent time together in the cramped kitchen on the bus. Teresa had found it to be a win-win. There was nothing more enjoyable than doing her favourite thing with her favourite person.

"I'm not getting arrested—even if your sausage is the reward." Hyde said the words so seriously that Teresa lost it.

She tried her hardest, but she dissolved into uncontrollable giggles. "I thought you loved my sausage."

"I… I am not entirely sure how to respond to that question." Hyde watched with a bewildered smile while Teresa tried to stop laughing. They snickered for a moment. "Stop it."

"I'm trying." Teresa coughed a few times, holding her side while leaning into Hyde. "Are you saying no to the sausage?"

Their laughter began all over again. It was a miracle they didn't wind up falling over. They clung to each other, snickering helplessly until their sides hurt and their voices were hoarse.

"I feel like I should caution the two of you for something, but I'm not sure what." Constable Trishna Jain had pulled up beside them. Her twin sister, Vidya, waved from the passenger's seat. "Are you all right?"

"Fine." Teresa managed to choke out the word. She breathed in deeply several times, attempting to control herself for a second time. "Just something silly. We're on our way to Al Dente."

"Have you been drinking?"

Teresa caught the teasing lilt of Trishna's voice, but she knew Hyde didn't when they tensed beside her. "This early in the day? We would never."

Trishna laughed with her twin before waving them on their way. "Sure you wouldn't. Go on, you two. Save us some pasta."

With a squeeze of Hyde's hand, Teresa nodded to the twin constables and led her ginger partner down the sidewalk. She knew the vampire would need a moment to process the interaction. They walked slowly and in a companionable silence.

It was already dark outside. The quaint village lamps flickered on, bathing the street in a warm glow. Teresa always admired the ancient magic used to create them. They were a beautiful marvel.

The weather had turned predictably frosty. Teresa was grateful for her thick leather jacket. Her long brown hair was blown around by the wind that had picked up as the day progressed, but thankfully there wasn't any rain.

Her Mexican half did not appreciate the cold, but her Irish blood thrilled at it. Teresa always felt closest to those ancestors in the winter. It didn't make any sense to her, yet she found those rituals and spells easier during the cooler months.

Magic had a mind of its own. It had been the first lesson her abuela had taught her. She'd encouraged Teresa to respect and honour both sets of ancestors. Each family had their own rituals, spells, and history.

Having been rejected by both sides of her family,

Teresa had made her home in South Myrddin. The one place, in what often felt like the entire world, where everyone was welcomed. She'd never regretted making the move, especially after meeting Hyde.

Hyde.

They'd become friends in a surprisingly short amount of time, bonding over a love of books and knitting. Hyde had welcomed Teresa into the Skeleton Crew. Though she had to pass the Mortar and Pestle test—the cats were more discerning than their vampire.

Teresa hadn't fallen in love slowly. It was almost embarrassing how quickly she'd gone from "I enjoy this vampire" to "I would wreck a fair amount of Scotland for them." *I'm being mildly dramatic, but only mildly.*

"You're talking to yourself again."

"I'm what?" Teresa was jolted out of her thoughts by a nudge from Hyde, who guided them both out of the path of a bench. "Talking to myself?"

"Not out loud. I can always tell. You frown." Hyde touched the tip of their finger to the side of her lips. "Right there. The 'I'm talking to myself' frown."

It was sweet and left-of-centre and completely Hyde. Teresa turned her head to kiss the tip of their finger. They rolled their eyes and dropped their hand back down.

"Was it a good conversation?" Hyde asked after a few seconds.

Teresa shook her head and laughed, groaning when her sides protested a little. "I was thinking about when I first arrived in the village."

"Second best day of my life. Beaten only by the day Mortar and Pestle came into it." Hyde stopped when they drew close to Al Dente. They could hear shouting from inside. "Sounds like it's going well."

3

HYDE

"Why don't you bugger off?" Amalia's voice carried above the chaos inside the restaurant.

"You invited us."

"No, I didn't," Amalia insisted.

Hyde didn't recognise the blonde woman who was shouting back at Amalia. They hesitated to walk fully into Al Dente. The atmosphere seemed more conducive to a brawl and indigestion as opposed to a celebration. "Have we come at a bad time?"

"No." Battista waved them inside. He came over to them, gleefully shoving two other strangers out of the way. His smile was brittle but genuine. "Ah. You've brought it, yes? Excellent. I've made your favourite stew to celebrate as promised."

Despite his many years in South Myrddin, Battista retained the soul and style of his beloved

New Orleans. He was dapper—always dressed to impress. His ancestors went back centuries amongst the Louisiana Creole demon coven. It had been Amalia's exile from her family that led both of them to make the journey to the Scottish Highlands.

The two were best friends and lovers. An incubus and a succubus. A relationship that shouldn't work yet did. It made Hyde question their belief in soulmates not existing. They were so opposite, brought together by their passionate zest for all the joys in life.

Amalia's red hair was a more auburn shade than Hyde's. Her amber eyes shone brightly. Battista had eyes as black as night that glowed when he was angry. His inky hair, currently hidden underneath one of his many hats, was closely trimmed and had a smattering of grey throughout.

Hyde held the book out to him. "It's the oldest manuscript I could find. It's obviously a later translation. I highly doubt the original scroll exists anywhere unless it's in some coven's vault."

"Thicker than I imagined." Battista carefully unwrapped the book. He let the brown paper fall to the ground while his gaze remained locked on the cover. His fingers trembled when they traced over the gold-embossed letters. "I can't believe you found it."

The arguing in the restaurant came to such a sudden stop that the silence was somehow louder. Hyde looked up to find Amalia weaving her way through her family. She came up behind Battista, gripping his arm tightly while she leaned in closer.

"It's exquisite." Amalia seemed to be holding her breath as Battista gingerly opened the book. He paused at the title page, which had a beautiful painting of an incubus and succubus. "I thought it would be a more slender edition."

"This is a collection of ancient Roman texts on incubus and succubus." Hyde had been lucky to find it at all. They'd used their connection with other bookshops and antique dealers across the world. "It includes the specific one you were hunting for, along with several others."

"You are magnificent." Amalia eyed the book reverently.

"Is she talking about me or the book?" Hyde whispered to Teresa, who snickered. They nudged her with their elbow, trying to hush her, when Battista and Amalia glanced up. "The translated title is *A Collection of Demonic Lust.* I believe the original Latin was simply *Daemonium et Libidine. Demons and Lust.* Or as close to the original as we're going to get at this point."

Battista carefully closed the book and offered it to

Amalia. She wrapped it in a heavy silk cloth and disappeared through the door leading to the kitchen. "We'll eat first, then inspect the text further. Thank you."

Hyde shrugged, uneasy with the intense attention from him and the strangers in the room. "Just my job."

"Nothing you do is merely your job." Battista gave their shoulder a quick squeeze. "You put immense effort into hunting down something precious to us. Accept our gratitude and praise."

"I'd rather accept snacks."

Battista laughed. It was a deep melodic sound that resonated in the room. "Snacks we can do. I've made a special version of our creole spaghetti, substituting the andouille we usually use for boudin noir—one of my family recipes for spiced blood sausage. You're going to love it."

Ignoring everyone else in the restaurant, Battista led them over to the large table in the centre of the room, the one they used for more family-style meals. Something they did in the village every so often.

Amalia had already brought out a few of the dishes after safely securing the book. "Our stracotto alla fiorentina, for those who want a hearty stew. There's also our roasted tomato and cheese focaccia with a wild garlic and rosemary-infused olive oil."

"Along with a selection of the other dishes from our menu." Battista returned from the kitchen with multiple platters in hand. He managed to get everything safely on the table without dropping any of the items. "Including the spaghetti."

Introductions happened once everyone was seated. Amalia's estranged family had shown up uninvited, according to her. Her father, brother, and sister-in-law all disagreed. They'd even shown the letter supposedly sent from her.

Hyde kept their attention focused on the delicious food and not the family powder keg across the table. They were one of two people who took a healthy portion of the spaghetti. "Smells delicious."

Despite some false stereotypes about vampires, Hyde gained sustenance from food as well as the bottled blood they drank. They smiled when Battista set a glass in front of them. It was hard not to dive into the food, waiting for everyone to settle down. Patience had never been their strongest virtue.

Amalia finally brought out the last plate. This one held Al Dente's locally famous steak and potato ravioli covered in a thick and creamy cheese sauce. It was the most decadent dish on the menu. "Here we are. Others in the village will come by later. For now, mangia!"

Hyde immediately went for the spaghetti. It was

as tasty as expected. A hint of spice that pricked at their mouth along with a rich tanginess of the sauce. "It's so…."

"Hyde?" Teresa twisted towards them when they trailed off. "Are you okay?"

Hyde tried to focus on Teresa, with the room beginning to spin violently. They dropped their fork. It clattered against the plate and drew attention from the rest of the table. "I can't."

A second fork fell. Hyde tried to turn their head, but a wave of nausea kept them staying as stationary as possible. Everything was so heavy on their body. They didn't understand what had happened.

"Hyde? Hyde." Teresa shook their shoulder, rushing out of her chair as they felt the world begin to tilt. "Hey? Hyde? I need you to take a breath for me."

"I feel… odd."

The shouts around them sounded garbled. Hyde was sinking into an ocean of nothingness. They tried to grab a hold of Teresa's hand before everything faded away.

4

TERESA

THE WORLD HAD SLOWED DOWN. TERESA LOWERED Hyde to the ground while screaming for someone to call for an ambulance. She heard Battista on the phone with Dr Wilfred Aniston, a druid who ran the local clinic. A wise choice since he'd likely arrive before the police or EMTs.

"Hyde?" Teresa's hands shook as she tried to make the vampire more comfortable. There were no signs of an allergic reaction, but something had clearly happened. "I don't know what to do. What should we do? I don't know what to do."

Her anxiety choked her. Teresa fluttered her hands, trying to shake off the impending attack. She had to stay present and focused to help Hyde.

Seconds seemed to tick by at an agonising pace. Battista knelt on the other side of Hyde. He gently bent over to listen to their chest before forcing their mouth open and peering inside.

In a flash of movement, Battista had yanked Hyde up to their feet. He wrapped his arms around them and began compressing their upper body with a violent amount of force. It took several tries for a chunk of sausage to fly out of their mouth.

"Were they poisoned?" Teresa rushed over to check on Hyde as Battista cradled them in a chair. "Was it poison?"

"Not poison. A curse. One I've seen before. Not an easy one to cast." Amalia had the platter of spaghetti in her hands. She was carefully inspecting it. "Hyde should be okay with the meat out of their throat."

"Your brother was not so lucky," Amalia's father spat viciously, gesturing to the body of Rocco Bassani on the ground.

"You killed him." Gia, Rocco's wife, launched herself at Amalia, only for Vitya to appear out of nowhere to grab her. "She killed him."

"I'm going to need everyone to calm down. Hamish is on the way. Pretty sure the doc is as well. I saw him jogging up the street." Constable Vitya Antonov provided much-needed order to the chaos. He turned his head to where Battista still held Hyde. "Are they breathing?"

"Barely." Battista nodded to the platter of spaghetti. "Someone did something to the pasta. I don't know what or who. It wasn't us. We certainly had no reason to want to hurt this precious one—and we made it for them specifically."

Before the conversation could devolve into another argument, the door slammed open. Emrys strode inside the restaurant with no sign of his usual jovial nature. Anger radiated around him as if lightning itself crackled from the tips of his fingers.

Of all the older villagers, Emrys took the care of the foundlings the most seriously. He was often the one who settled them into new homes. Hyde, however, had always been a firm favourite of his.

Relatively speaking, Teresa had come to South Myrddin later in life than most. Hyde had arrived as a child. They'd basically been raised by the village— and Emrys.

"What happened?'" Emrys spoke quietly into the chaos. The weight of his words silenced everyone. "I asked a question."

"While you get an answer, Battista can assist me in getting Hyde outside. Hamish should be here in the ambulance shortly." Wilfred had arrived relatively quickly and brooked absolutely no argument. He glowered at Vitya, who held up his hands. "Let's go. I want to make certain they're okay."

A tense silence filled the room until the trio had left the restaurant. Once the door closed, Amalia's remaining family immediately screamed at her. Their accusations drowned out everyone else attempting to speak.

"Someone tried to commit vampire-cide, and I want to know who it was." Teresa cursed loudly in Spanish, cutting through the arguing, waving her hands about wildly until Emrys came over to her. She tried to take a deep breath to calm her racing heart, clinging to anger instead of panic. He wrapped an arm around her shoulders and pulled her away. "They could've died."

"Hyde is going to be fine," Emrys stated with such absolute certainty that it calmed her a little. "And I *will* find out who attempted to harm a foundling in my village."

"Emrys. We don't know what happened."

Completely ignoring the note of warning in Vitya's voice, Emrys guided Teresa out of the restaurant. News had spread across the village. A crowd had already gathered to help where they could, which included Hamish and his ambulance.

"See? Wilfred and Hamish will make sure Hyde is okay." Emrys gave her shoulders a squeeze. He frowned when he glanced over to their left. "Why don't you head to the ambulance and check on them? I've got someone I want a word with."

Teresa nodded. She watched Emrys make his way through the crowd to Chief Inspector Jonatan Pacheco. *Shite.* "Not my problem."

Leaving Emrys to handle the prickly vampire elder, Teresa headed for the ambulance. A decidedly grumpy Hyde sat on the bed inside with Wilfred and Hamish fussing over them. It would've been amusing if not for the circumstances.

Hamish Keir was a gentle giant. A bear of a man who'd once played rugby for the Scottish national team. He preferred life as an EMT, though he spent much of his time in and around South Myrddin, claiming it was better for his anxiety to be in a familiar place.

Wilfred and Hamish finally stepped back, allowing Teresa to move closer. The doctor whispered something to the EMT before he left the ambulance. She watched him head over to speak with Emrys and the police.

"I'm okay," Hyde grumbled. Their voice was scratchy and quiet. Teresa noticed their body trembled slightly despite the blanket draped across their legs. "I'm not sure I'm a fan of boudin noir. It seems to be hazardous to my health."

"Hyde." Teresa sat on the fold-down chair across from them. "How are you feeling?"

"Oddly happy to not have been poisoned. A curse doesn't require the blasted activated charcoal." Hyde dramatically pretended to retch for a moment. "I'd almost rather have a stake through my heart than drink the stuff again."

"Better drinking it and living than staying poisoned," Hamish unhelpfully pointed out. "I'm going to have a quick word with Emrys. He's got the most experience with flushing curses out of the body."

Teresa turned to the side and leaned back, allowing Hamish to squeeze by her. She shifted forward once he was gone and took Hyde's hand. "How are you really?"

"Floaty. My ribs hurt. I can't blame Battista, though."

"Floaty?"

"It's all so much. My brain can't process it. Feels like I've had wool shoved into my ears, and every-thing's muted." Hyde picked at the blanket over their legs. "Not how I imagined our date going."

"Not how anyone imagined the dinner going."

"Sorry you didn't get to enjoy the stew. I know you were looking forward to it."

"Bugger the stew." Teresa gave them a pointed look. "And no, I don't mean literally."

"Have they said anything about Rocco Bassani?"

"Not yet." Teresa had almost forgotten about him. She wondered how Amalia was handling the death of her brother, even if they'd been estranged. It had been easier to focus on Hyde. "Probably won't tell us anything even if we ask."

"Why would someone poison him—or me?"

It was hard not to think about the poison attempt a few weeks back. Hyde had eaten a tainted pastry left at the bookshop. They'd been violently ill but thankfully not otherwise unharmed.

The poison had been left by the same man who'd killed Florence—a warlock named Angus Peck. It had been a relief when the police caught up with him. The man had confessed to the murder and was now spending the rest of his life in a warded prison cell.

Though Angus had never confessed to any additional crimes, Teresa firmly believed he'd been behind the attempt to poison Hyde at the time. She was glad Emrys had ensured he could never escape from prison. Warlocks were among the most dangerous magic wielders—not the strongest. Still, they certainly leaned towards more harm than good, unlike their druid counterparts.

"Resa?"

"Hmm?" Teresa shoved the memories away and focused on Hyde in the present. "Something wrong? You need Hamish back?"

"No. How would someone place a curse on the food with all of us there?" Hyde lowered their voice while their gaze flicked from Teresa to the open ambulance doors, checking to see if anyone was in hearing range. "Theoretically, I'd assume only the chefs would have access. But there's no way Amalia or Battista tried to hurt me—and they made the dish for me. So, who did it? And who was the target?"

"Aside from you?"

"Aside from you, Amalia, and Battista, no one in that room knows me." Hyde had an excellent point. The uninvited guests had all been strangers. "Were they trying to kill someone and frame Amalia or Battista for it?"

"No, no, we're not investigating this." Teresa knew it was only a token resistance. She was admittedly just as curious now that the danger to her vampire had passed. "Hyde."

"What if they arrest Amalia? It was her brother who died. And we know she was estranged from her family. They'll claim she wanted revenge." Hyde sat up on the bed, waving off Teresa's worry. "I am fine.

Wilfred and Hamish cleared away any of the curse's residue."

"Let's wait and see what happens." Teresa helped Hyde get to their feet. She smiled when the vampire wrapped the blanket around their shoulders. "Not sure the doctor would approve."

"Oh, balls."

"What?" Teresa turned, following Hyde's gaze to see two of the village constables leading Amalia towards a waiting vehicle. "Bugger."

"They're going to arrest her."

"Hyde." Teresa tried to grab them by the shoulder. "Hyde. We don't know why they were leading her away."

"It wasn't to exchange recipes." Hyde pressed forward determinedly. They dodged Vitya when he tried to stop them from entering the restaurant. "Where is he?"

"Hyde." Vitya had clearly been told to remain by the doors to keep people out. He cursed under his breath before glaring at Teresa. "Stop them."

"Have you ever attempted to stop a vampire? You probably have. You have shifter strength. I'm a witch. I can do many things with spells and rituals, but stopping a stubborn vampire isn't on the list of my abilities." Teresa couldn't help the slight smile while she watched the ginger vampire storm towards their nemesis. "Doesn't a little part of you want to see them rip into Pacheco just once?"

Vitya pressed his lips tightly together to avoid grinning. "I can neither confirm nor deny."

5

HYDE

Hyde found the illustrious chief inspector in the middle of a heated conversation with Battista. They strode right over and shoved him in the back. "Amalia wouldn't try to kill me. Neither would Battista. What the blazes are you doing? You absolute berk."

"I am going to pretend you didn't just physically and verbally assault a police officer."

"Fine. I'll do it again." Hyde was stopped by Emrys coming over to wrap an arm around their shoulders. "The tainted dish was made for me. Are you honestly going to say Amalia tried to kill me? Someone tampered with it after it was made."

"And all your years of police work gave you this grand insight?" Chief Inspector Pacheco had always been a thorn in their side, or perhaps it was vice versa. He had never approved of Hyde because they refused to be a good little vampire. "We haven't arrested anyone. Amalia has been detained. Questions have to be asked."

"Oh."

"Yes, oh. Would you like us to make an arrest? I have witnesses who will say you shoved me." He smiled toothily, his fangs on full display. "You're supposed to be in the ambulance."

"I didn't see a thing." Emrys's smirk was equally steely. "You obviously lost your balance."

"I've recovered. Hamish said I needed rest," Hyde interjected before the two men could go at each other.

"So, the logical choice was to come into the scene of the crime and shove me?" Pacheco asked.

"It got your attention." Hyde folded their arms across their chest and continued to glower at the man who loomed over them. "They put her into the back of a police car. You didn't put anyone else there."

"Would you prefer she ride on top?"

"That's not... she might enjoy it." Hyde shook her head, trying not to get distracted by the visual. "She didn't try to kill me."

"First, no one has said she did. Second, the target of the curse or poison could've been anyone at the table. Third, I am not explaining myself to a civilian."

Pacheco had taken another step closer. His jaw was clenched tightly. He seemed like a rubber band stretched a little too far and poised to snap. "You are not a detective, despite your best efforts to interfere in the investigation into Florence's death."

"A lengthy explanation for someone not doing so." Emrys eased his way into the conversation, taking the heat off Hyde, who had started to feel light-headed at diving headfirst into a confrontation. "A little snark and anger but still plenty of details."

"Druid." Pacheco's full attention shifted to Emrys.

"Vampire."

It was a clash of village titans. The cold-as-ice vampire with his blue eyes, perfectly styled greying hair, trimmed beard, and tall, strong frame. Vincent Pacheco always appeared as though he'd stepped off a Spanish fashion magazine.

Emrys, on the other hand, had the weathered, aged look of an ancient fisherman. His tousled white hair and scruffy beard always appeared windswept. His blue eyes held a touch of warmth. He radiated power, calm, and wisdom—the perfect druid.

"Leave my foundlings alone." Emrys gave Hyde's shoulder a squeeze before turning them towards Teresa. "Why don't you two lovebirds finish your date at the bookshop? I'll swing by later or in the morning to make sure none of the curse lingers."

"I have questions," the chief inspector protested.

Emrys placed a hand on Pacheco's chest. "Questions that can wait until later. Off you pop, foundling."

For a brief second, Hyde found themselves adrift. It was like floating on the loch with their head half underwater. Everything around them was muffled, even the growing argument between Emrys and the chief inspector.

"How about we see if Rosa has any baked goods left before she closes up shop? We can nibble by the fire," Teresa suggested. She waited patiently while Hyde attempted to process her words.

Rosa Pacheco wasn't any more fond of her uncle than Hyde. She ran The Golden Puff. It was the village bakery, which had all number of delightful savoury and sweet treats.

"I need to sit down." Hyde wrapped their arms around their upper body to hide the trembling. They walked quickly away from the restaurant, dodging and weaving around the still-gathered onlookers. Teresa jogged to keep up with them. "I have to go home."

"We'll get you there. It's not far."

"Nothing in the village is far. We have what, six

roads at most? The loch is bigger than the village," Hyde muttered. Even their voice felt too loud in their head. They tried to block everything out and keep moving. "Sorry."

"Don't. You've had a rough evening." Teresa kept pace with them easily, which wasn't difficult since she was taller. She also deflected a few well-meaning friends with a wave of her hand and a nod towards Hyde. "Amalia's going to be fine."

"I shoved him. And I yelled at him."

"I saw. It was glorious. I might commission artwork to commemorate and savour the moment for the rest of our lives."

"Resa." Hyde chuckled weakly. "I'm not sure he found it quite as amusing."

"Hello, little cub." Reuben Rutherford strode across the street towards them. His presence chased off anyone lingering nearby, wanting to question them. He slipped over to Hyde's other side. "Why don't you lean on me until we get back to the bookshop? You look about five seconds away from coming apart at the seams."

If the village had an alpha, it was Reuben. He'd come to the village as a young man the year before Hyde. They'd always been close. He treated them like a younger sibling.

As a werewolf, Reuben believed firmly in the

concept of family and pack. He ran The Den—a village boarding house for werewolves and shifters without a home. A safe space that he hadn't had until he'd moved to South Myrddin.

Werewolves and vampires weren't often the closest of friends. Reuben tended to keep as far away from them as possible aside from Hyde. They were definitely the exception in his eyes.

Taller and stronger than any of the other wolves or shifters in the village, no one messed with Reuben. Hyde always thought of him as a gentle giant. But they were biased.

"I'll jog over to the bakery. You know Rosa will have saved something for us, if only to spite her uncle." Teresa gave their arm a squeeze before racing across the street.

"All right, cub. Let's get you home to your cats and books." Reuben didn't touch them and kept a sliver of space between them as they walked. "Hamish cleared you?"

Hyde nodded.

"Good. I brought you back a treasure from my hunt." Reuben reached into the pocket of his coat. He held out a hardbound book to them. "I happened on this outdoor market after spending a few weeks in the mountains. This was there."

"Oh," Hyde exclaimed softly. *"An Illustrated Book of Autumn."*

The cover was a faded green with embossed leaves, and the faint hint of gold still clung to the letters. They gingerly opened the first pages to find a stunning hand-painted illustration of a Japanese maple in full autumn splendour. The book was full of similar paintings.

"It's from the 1870s, I think. A good find. Not one I think you have in your nature collection." Reuben guided them away from the lamppost when they almost walked into it. "You devour books like I do steak."

"Not literally. They'd taste dusty and of ink." Hyde made a face. They still sensed the impending need to release energy to prevent a full-blown melt-down, but the distraction had helped. "I thought you'd be gone for another month."

"Heard someone tried to topple a tree onto your head."

Hyde shrugged.

"Tell me all about it later, cub." Reuben remained silent for the rest of the short walk to the bookshop. He opened the door for them when the keys fell out of their hand. "In you go. Mortar and Pestle will take good care of you."

Hyde took the keys when he handed them over. "Okay."

"Give me a howl if the self-important fanged elder gives you any trouble." Reuben went over to make sure the fire was going, then left the bookshop, closing the door quietly behind him.

Hyde dragged their hand along the counter, bumping against each groove in the wood. They flipped the Talk sign over to Shh. "Blasted berk."

Energy boiled up inside them where they'd tried to shove it away. It itched under their skin. They shook their hands vigorously in an attempt to keep from scratching themselves.

Berk.

Repeating the word over and over, Hyde hopped around the shop, trying to rid themselves of the pent-up anxious energy. They flopped onto the armchair by the fire. Exhaustion warred with the rush of confused adrenaline.

Hyde grabbed a cushion and screamed into it until the crawling sensation under their skin went away. "Hello, kitties."

Motor and Pestle had stalked over to them. They leapt up onto the armchair, curling up in Hyde's lap. Their fur was silky soft against their fingers.

The soothing rumbling of their purrs smoothed the raw edges left over from the meltdown. Hyde was almost drifting off when the front door opened. Teresa called out a quiet hello.

Hyde carefully leaned forward to see around the edge of the armchair. "Croissants?"

"Rosa had quite a few leftovers. She'd heard about what happened at Al Dente. Made up all your favourites, plus a thermos of one of her calming tea blends. The one she claims works when her uncle is being… his usual self. She also promised to tell him off when she sees him next." Teresa kept her voice low. She made her way over to the cosy corner in front of the fire, setting the thermos and large box on the small coffee table. "I'll grab a couple mugs and plates. Want me to put on one of your records?"

Hyde managed a nod.

"How about Away with the Faeries?" Teresa asked after picking through the collection of records. "Nice acoustic, mellow folk?"

"Okay."

Taking that as a yes, Teresa put on the record. She went over to the tea cabinet and grabbed their mugs, bringing them over with a couple of small plates. Hyde stared blankly at the fire, letting its warmth and the soothing music wash over them.

After a few minutes of thawing out from an emotional numbness, Hyde reached out to grasp the mug. They sipped their way through half of the calming tea before grabbing one of the pastries.

Xuixo was one of Rosa's specialities. It was a roll of deep-fried pastry filled with cream and sprinkled with cinnamon sugar. She always claimed it was as if a croissant and a churro had a love child. Hyde tried not to visualise that description whenever they ate them.

Three pastries and a large mug of tea later, Hyde regained some semblance of themselves. Words still didn't want to form. Teresa was thankfully content to cuddle together with them and the cats, listening to music and the crackling fire.

Another mug of tea helped. Hyde had no idea what exactly went into Rosa's calming blend. It might affect how it worked to learn the magic behind it.

Hyde leaned forward to set their empty mug on the coffee table. "I shouldn't have shoved him."

"Lies. You definitely should've shoved him even harder. It was glorious." Teresa perked up. She lifted Mortar out of her lap and placed the cat into Hyde's. "I wouldn't do it on a regular basis, but there were extenuating circumstances, which anyone could understand."

"He won't."

"When has Chief Inspector Pacheco ever understood anything about you or anyone other than his club of uptight vampires?" Teresa stretched her arm out, wrapping it around Hyde's shoulders. "Are you feeling better?"

"Mildly." Hyde shifted so their head rested more comfortably against Teresa. "Battista and Amalia wouldn't try to kill me—even accidentally."

"No, they wouldn't."

Hyde was relieved at how confident Teresa sounded. It dismissed any feint lingering doubts in the back of their mind. "So, someone in the restaurant managed to curse the dish."

"If it wasn't them or us, it leaves two other people."

"Or the victim himself. What if he mixed up which dish it was?" Hyde knew it was a stretch, but it was possible. "Could someone have snuck into the kitchen while we were all in the dining room?"

"Without Battista or Amalia noticing?" Teresa stared mournfully into the empty box of pastries. "I should've gotten more. These aren't even touching the sides. Want tacos?"

"Maybe Rees will have pity on us and fry up some fish and chips." Hyde glanced down when their stomach grumbled loudly. "Would you notice if someone had been in your kitchen?"

"Probably." Teresa got slowly to her feet, clearly

reluctant to leave the warmth. "Though, truthfully, if there were no signs of a break-in, I can't say for certain that I would."

"So, we have the father, the wife, or some random person who snuck into the kitchen?" Hyde unravelled themselves from all the blankets and dislodged a grumpy Mortar. She slunk over to Pestle, curling up together. "Why would they want to kill him?"

"Or you."

"I was collateral damage."

"Only you could be collateral damage to cursed spaghetti." Teresa laughed when Hyde threw a napkin at her. "Are you up for going out? I can pick up dinner for us."

"I am. I'm…." Hyde paused to consider. They definitely had the tired, almost hungover feeling from a meltdown, but they thought a short walk might do them good. "It'll be fine."

"Well, you can always shove anyone who annoys you." Teresa snickered when Hyde glowered at her. "It might help."

"I'm eating your chips," Hyde grumbled. "You shove one person, and no one lets you forget it."

"First, it's just me. Second, you shoved Pacheco, not a random person." Teresa looped her arm with Hyde's and led them towards the door. "I'll get you an extra portion of chips as a reward."

6

TERESA

THE CLOSER THEY GOT TO THE DOOR, THE MORE hesitant Hyde became. Teresa waited patiently. They checked the counter, the cats, and even returned to inspect the doused fire.

Teresa knew the delaying tactics well. She was often absolutely shattered after a panic attack, and a meltdown had to be equally physically and emotionally exhausting. "Hyde?"

"I'm… ready."

"How about I pick our supper up? Rees knows your favourites. I won't even have to order." Teresa slipped her arms around Hyde for a quick yet gentle embrace. She dropped a kiss on their forehead before stepping back. "Go on upstairs and get comfy. We can eat while we catch up on the latest episode of the *Hags of London*."

"Fine," Hyde grumbled.

They both occasionally enjoyed the guilty pleasure of watching silly shows.

Teresa gave them one last peck on the lips before darting out of the shop. She was pleased to see that the villagers seemed to have dispersed.

As Teresa walked up the lane towards Malt Moon, she noticed caution tape still around Al Dente. The coroner's van had left, but plenty of police vehicles remained. She could see a distraught Battista in conversation with Detective Inspector Baines through the windows.

Fynn spotted her through the window and headed out of the restaurant. He jogged over to catch up with her. "How's Jekyll?"

"Pulling into their shell like a tortoise. They'll be fine in the morning, I think." Teresa nodded towards the restaurant. "Is Battista okay?"

"Angry that we've taken Amalia in for questioning. I can't tell you anything else. And you try to keep your nose out of the investigation. Both of you." Fynn, unlike his boss, always seemed to greatly enjoy Hyde. "Something's not quite right about this case. Try to stay away, will you?"

"I'll do my best."

"Baines," Pacheco shouted from the restaurant. He glared when he spotted Teresa.

"Better go. He's still annoyed at being told off by Hyde and Emrys." Fynn winked at her before racing back to the restaurant; his dreadlocks flew behind him.

The detective, who had moved to Scotland from Wales after his father's passing, had inherited his Ghanaian mother's ability to see both the past and future with varying degrees of clarity. Teresa took his word of caution seriously. She wasn't sure how convinced Hyde would be, though, when she found out Amalia was still being questioned.

Continuing up the lane, Teresa found Rees about to close up shop. She glanced at her watch. It was a bit early; he tended to stay open a little later than most.

"Any chance of grabbing something before you close?" Teresa was relieved to see he hadn't shut down any of his equipment yet. "Hyde's feeling a bit peckish."

"Are they? Everything all right? Heard they had a row with Chief Inspector Pillock." Rees grinned when Teresa burst out laughing. "The whole village is talking about it—along with Rocco's death, of course. Says something about how out of character the shove was for them to be gossiping about it over the sad loss of Amalia's brother."

"Hyde's going to hate that. They're already feeling guilty about it."

"Tell them not to bother. The pillock deserved it. Now, fish, a couple of extra-large packets of extra-crispy chips, and I'm guessing battered blutwurst for the little duck." Rees moved efficiently around the small kitchen behind the counter. "Oh, tell them Emrys took the cursed letters. He's going to see what he can sniff out—probably not literally, though you never know with druids."

In no time at all, Rees had handed over multiple packets of food. He sent her on her way, promising to keep them updated on the letter situation. Teresa juggled the packets a little until they were easier to carry.

With the food in hand, she retraced her steps to the bookshop. She couldn't help glancing at Al Dente on the way past. The lights were out, the doors shut, and caution tape had been wrapped around the handles.

The police vehicles had all gone. Teresa wondered if Battista and Amalia were okay. There were no signs of them or Amalia's father and sister-in-law. Perhaps they were all being questioned by the police.

Like many of the shops in the village, Amalia and Battista lived in the flat above the restaurant. Teresa didn't see any lights on inside. It made her think they were definitely at the police station.

She was reaching for the bookshop door handle when she heard footsteps. She groaned internally when she turned to see who'd approached her so late in the evening. "Chief Inspector."

"I have a few questions for both you and Mx Snodgrass." He was as stony-faced as ever. His expression gave nothing away. "I'd prefer to wrap them up this evening."

"Good for you. Hyde's not up for questions, so why don't you come back in the morning. Or better yet, maybe send Fynn, since he's less likely to irritate Hyde." Teresa refused to be intimidated even when he loomed over her. "It's not happening tonight unless you plan on forcing your way into the bookshop."

"I'm the chief inspector."

"And? Nothing is going to change if you ask your questions in the morning." Teresa didn't think Hyde would be able to give him answers. The day and the meltdown had taken a lot out of them. "You can wait."

"Fine. I'll be back in the morning."

She watched him stalk away. He vanished into the darkness after a moment. "Berk."

Making her way into the bookshop, Teresa

wondered how warrants worked for vampire cops. She made sure to lock up before heading upstairs. Hyde was cosily ensconced on the plush rug on the floor, wrapped in blankets, and covered by cats.

"Theoretically speaking, if a vampire detective wasn't invited into a home, could they enter with a search warrant?" Teresa asked. She handed Hyde the food packets and then sat beside them, pulling the coffee table closer to set their dinner on. "Does legality overcome it?"

"That's a myth. I don't need an invitation to go into most places. Though, in theory, it might work on sacred spaces." Hyde picked through the packets until they found the chips and curry sauce. They grabbed their blutwurst as well. "Emrys did extensive research into rituals restricting vampires."

"Did he?"

"Ages ago. Before I came to the village. He had to make a change to allow me into his cottage." Hyde munched on a chip, breaking off a piece for Pestle when he perked up in their lap. "Not sure if it's a universal thing or if he did it to annoy Pacheco. He's never admitted to it."

Making themselves comfortable, they switched on the telly to watch *Hags of London*. Hyde tended to fixate on shows or music or books for a while, then move on to something else. Lately, it had been reality television, which Teresa thought was mostly for them to observe bizarre behaviour of the non-autistic.

After supper had finished and the show was over, Hyde switched on a classical music concert. They settled in beside Teresa. It was a lovely, relaxing end to a chaotic and stressful day.

Teresa sighed when she remembered her conversation outside the bookshop. It wouldn't do to have Hyde surprised. "Pacheco has questions for us."

Hyde immediately groaned. They twisted their head to hide their face against Teresa's shoulder. "Why? Why me? What gods have I offended? Is this because we didn't swim naked in the loch?"

"It is not because we didn't swim naked in the loch to celebrate Florence's death with Flossie and Winnie. And thank you for reminding me. I'd tried to blot it out of my memory." Teresa snickered at the second dramatic groan that was muffled by her shirt. "We were at the dinner. I would've been surprised if the police didn't have more questions for us. Maybe we can talk Emrys into hanging around when Pacheco shows up. He can keep Chief Inspector Berk in line for us."

"Mmm." Hyde cuddled closer into her, getting more comfortable. "Is it a nap if it's late at night? Because I could use a nap.'

"A bat nap, maybe."

"You are horrible." Hyde poked her in the side. "I am not a bat. That's a myth."

"I bet Chief Inspector Berk hangs upside from the rafters."

"He has a fancy coffin lined with silk. A family heirloom. I think it's gold plated or something." Hyde stared serenely back at Teresa, who was absolutely gobsmacked.

"Seriously?"

"No, of course not." Hyde dissolved into helpless giggles when Teresa shoved them over. "Do I need to get you a *Vampires 101: Things to Know When Dating One* book?"

7

HYDE

The irony of the witch in their relationship being the one to sleep like the dead wasn't lost on Hyde. They'd woken up to banging on the front door while Teresa continued to snore. It had taken a moment to process what the sound was.

Hyde stumbled down the stairs into the bookshop. It was barely eight in the morning. They fumbled with the lock before managing to open the door. "You."

"I have a few questions about yesterday. You were told to expect me."

"It's too early for you to be your normal berkish self." Hyde glared at Pacheco's top button. They sighed after a moment and stepped back to let him into the shop. "What questions do you have?"

Wandering into the shop, Pacheco inspected the

nearest shelf. Hyde rolled their eyes and turned their attention to the signs on the counter. They flipped the Shh to Hello but left the They alone.

Pacheco picked up one of the latest finds from their rare book hunts. He inspected it carefully before returning it to the shelf. "Our magical forensic team is still documenting and dissecting the curse placed on the pasta. They've already determined it was a rare one."

"Was there a question in there?" Hyde fidgeted with the string on their pyjama bottoms. They were handmade, designed to be like vintage pinstripe ones. "I didn't hear it."

"Do you remember anyone being near the bowl of spaghetti?"

"It was a platter," Hyde muttered pedantically. They ducked their head down, hiding a smile when he sighed loudly. "Bowls have rounder and higher rims."

"Do you remember anyone being near the *platter* of spaghetti?" He practically growled out the last two words.

"Aside from literally everyone at the table, including myself?" Hyde wasn't trying to be difficult on purpose. His question didn't really help them figure out what he was looking for. "Everyone went near it for the brief moments it was on the table. No one cursed it in front of me. Do succubi or incubi perform rituals or have some other manner of it? How would theirs work?"

Ignoring his huff of frustration, Hyde wandered over to one of the nonfiction shelves. It held a selection of encyclopaedias on creatures, magic, and species. Some tomes were more accurate than others. They varied by age as well. It had taken years for them to build the collection.

"Do you know of any reason Amalia would've wanted to hurt her family?" Pacheco asked. "You were obviously not the target." He tapped his fingers impatiently while they hunted for the right book. "Hyde?"

"No." Hyde had initially assumed the curse was intended for them since the dish had been made with them in mind. But it stood to reason that the killer could've known Rocco Bassani's tastes were similar. Was it a genuine coincidence? "Not really."

"Not really?"

"I don't believe Amalia did this," Hyde stated firmly.

"But?"

"Theoretically speaking, any foundling in this village could drum up the motivation to lash out at the family who abandoned them." Hyde slammed a book back into place on the shelf. They stroked the spine gently as an apology. "The exiled. The thrown away. We can all find a reason. It doesn't mean we would."

Pacheco's sigh was more tired this time. "Families and covens may have reasons for the decisions they make. It might be difficult to hear or hard to stomach, but sometimes it's the best for everyone involved."

"Get out of my bookshop." Hyde clenched their fists at their sides. "You have never once tried to understand how it feels."

For the most part, Hyde was someone incredibly slow to anger. They didn't like the spike of adrenaline that came with extreme emotions. But the conflict with Pacheco had been building for years, decades even.

"Hyde."

"I'll answer questions from Fynn." Hyde moved away from the bookshelf. They went over to retrieve the Snodgrass grimoire from the locked box behind the counter. "I've read through this in the past couple of weeks."

"And?" He seemed confused by the slight change in subject.

"You knew my family."

"I did. I've never hidden that fact from you."

"You knew them incredibly well. Intimately even, if the notes are correct. And you knew they abandoned a child." Hyde had tried to come to terms with the knowledge for days.

"I disapproved."

"Did you? The great elder vampire. The coven leader over Europe. Disapproved." Hyde had allowed the hurt to simmer since the grimoire had been sent to them weeks ago. "And yet you did nothing to help."

"I don't intervene in family—" He cut himself off as though he knew it was the wrong thing to say.

"What is the point of a coven if it's not to intervene to protect a child?" Hyde sneered at him. "The veneer of propriety hides a lot of shame, Chief Inspector Pacheco. Ah, that's right. You are also a police officer. Top man. In charge of detectives."

"Hyde."

"You are no longer welcome in my home." Hyde gripped the grimoire tightly in their arms. "I don't understand you. Maybe I never will. You consistently fail the most vulnerable in your coven—even your own family, Rosa. And that is what I wished I'd said to you years and years ago. You failed. And you compounded your failure by being cruelly dismissive and judgemental of how we choose to live our lives."

"I tried my best to look out for you. Both you and Rosa." He hesitated by the door with his hand on the doorknob. "To make sure you settled in okay."

"How? By constantly disapproving of our decisions? I am who I am. I'm not changing for anyone—not even you. You can't mould us into perfect vampire clones. We're not made of clay." Hyde was suddenly more exhausted than words could express. They'd had so much hope for the day. "I would very much like you to leave."

"I'll send Detective Baines to speak with you later." Pacheco was oddly subdued. He shut the door quietly behind him when he left.

Hyde slumped into the nearest armchair. They discarded the grimoire, not wanting to hold it any longer. "Balls."

A gentle chime by the door let Hyde know one of the druids had come to visit. They dragged themselves out of the chair and slumped over to answer. Emrys's empathetic gaze was almost too much to bear.

"I saw Jonatan stalking away." Emrys opened his arms, waiting for Hyde to decide. They hesitated before falling into his embrace. "I'm sorry, foundling. He's never quite grasped how much misery he unintentionally heaps onto those already dealt a cruel hand."

Nodding, Hyde tried not to sniffle. They breathed in the comfort of Emrys. He, as always, smelled of a spring garden after a light rain, as if flowered vines were woven through his wild white beard.

"I shouted at him."

"I can't recall you ever raising your voice in all the decades I've known you." Emrys was smiling when they finally eased out of his arms. "I'm sure he deserved it."

Hyde pointed to the grimoire. "This mentions him."

"I'm not surprised. Jonatan has been the vampire leader for well over a century or more. Despite his failures in our beloved village, he does well with his coven." Emrys wandered over to the fireplace. A wave of his hand and a few murmured words had the flames reignited, dancing merrily. He turned his attention to the twinkling lights above the shelves, which also brightened a little more. "There we go. A little less gloom for us."

"He knew my parents. My family. About me."

Emrys held his hands out in front of the fire. He warmed them in silence for a while. "Hurtful, but not a surprise. It might explain why he treats you like Rosa as opposed to ignoring you."

Hyde slumped into the armchair closest to the fire. They grabbed the grimoire and hugged it to them. "I didn't answer any of his questions."

"I'm sure one of the other detectives is just as

capable. He'll likely leave you be for a while. You've given him a lot to think over." Emrys twisted around, still smiling at them. "Vampires are slow to change their minds."

"Hey," Hyde grumbled. "Don't paint us all with the same brush. I could say all druids are a few trees short of a forest."

"That's not a saying—and it's also probably true. Our communing with the earth does have an effect on us." He produced a pipe from his pocket. "May I?

"No." Hyde was unmoved by his pleading gaze. "You're not making my books smell like pipe."

"Fine, fine." Emrys sighed dramatically. "You might be interested to know the curse on the spaghetti is different from the one on the letters. I don't believe either Amalia or Battista tried to hurt anyone, especially you. It would require a level of malice that they're not capable of."

"Did you tell the detectives?"

"They, and I quote, 'require more than a druid's instincts,' at least, apparently, when it comes to motivation and intent." He scratched absently at his beard, canting his head to the side while deep in thought. "Amalia was still being questioned when I left the police station. I'm sure she'll be home in no time at all."

Teresa trudged into the bookshop with both cats

trailing after her. She paused in the doorway, glancing between Emrys and Hyde. "Has something happened?"

"They unloaded decades of justified anger at Chief Inspector Pacheco," Emrys answered, gesturing grandly towards Hyde with a bow. "Well deserved. I am on my way home. It's been a tiring night. Try to stay out of trouble, will you?"

"Do I want to know what happened?" Teresa watched Emrys leave as she dragged her fingers through her long brown hair before deftly pulling it together in a loose braid. "How about I get changed quickly and whip us up something for breakfast?"

"Chief Inspector Berk and I had a meeting of the minds." Hyde thought it was the mildest way of explaining their morning conversation with him. They glanced at the clock on the wall behind the counter. "It's early enough. I don't have to open yet. We could see what's on the menu at Roasted and Toasted."

"Oh, yes. I heard Trishna mention they'd gotten Shikoba a special chai blend. I'm hoping it's already in the mix." Teresa darted over, dodging Pestle and the coffee table, to give Hyde a kiss. "See you in ten?"

"Twenty. The cats will want their morning sacrifice." Hyde smiled when Mortar gave a particularly plaintive yowl. "See?"

"Ah, yes, must offer sustenance to the furry gods and goddesses." Teresa winked before jauntily making her way out of the shop.

Hyde watched her go before bending down to lift Mortar with a sigh. She rubbed her furry head against their chin. "I know, I know. I had to fall in love with a morning person. I suppose we can forgive her one great fault. Just not normal—being so vibrant and joyous before coffee."

8

TERESA

Roasted and Toasted was the lone coffee shop in the village, on Harbour Road beyond the bookshop and close to Selkie Street. Shikoba Apanni had opened it a few years earlier when they'd come to Scotland by way of Louisiana and the Choctaw Nation. Battista had been the one to recommend South Myrddin to them.

Shikoba was a two-spirited eagle shifter. They were also one of Hyde and Teresa's favourite people. They exuded calm and peace.

Teresa had always theorised that a person tended to be somewhat connected to their shifter nature. Shikoba, as an eagle, had a grace, wisdom, and quite strength to them. They also had a keen eye for trouble.

It was a gloomy, cold morning when they walked

through the village to Roasted and Toasted. Hyde trudged along beside Teresa. They were definitely going to need something to pick them up.

"Morning, you two." Shikoba had their long inky-black hair tied back. It showed off the bold tattoos on their neck and shoulders. "I've got a special treat for you."

"Oh?" Hyde leaned tiredly against the counter. "My morning has already involved an intense argument. I would very much like a special treat."

"Poor vampire." Shikoba ducked down and rummaged around under the counter. "Ah. Found them."

They held up two matching to-go mugs, which had painted fangs and tacos dancing on the front. Hyde snorted loudly when they saw it.

"Had these made especially for you two. Bring them in when you want coffee or tea. In fact, I've got a new vanilla chai hot chocolate. It's caffeinated and delicious. It'll wake you right up." Shikoba carried the mugs off. "Also, I've made blackberry balsamic and brie grilled cheese sandwiches this morning. Something a little sweet and savoury to round out your breakfast."

They munched on the sandwiches while nattering about the fatal dinner from the previous night. Shikoba mentioned seeing Battista without Amalia at

Al Dente. The caution tape had finally been removed from the doors.

With their mugs of chai in hand, Hyde and Teresa waved goodbye to Shikoba. Their curiosity led them towards the Italian restaurant. There was a lone light visible in the back, but no one answered their knocking.

"Maybe he's asleep?" Hyde tapped on the window a second time. They tried to give the door a pull, but it was locked. "I could break this, though I don't want to wreck it. Maybe we can give Battista a call?"

"Not getting into trouble, are we?" Fynn jogged across the street to stand beside them. "He's fine. I just saw him. Let him have some time to himself before you badger him with questions. Are we feeling better this morning?"

Hyde shrugged.

"They gave Chief Inspector Pacheco a bit of a bollocking this morning. I'm sad to have missed it." Teresa snickered when Hyde sighed loudly. "What? If one does magical things, one must take credit for them."

"Well done, Jekyll." Fynn winked at Hyde, who rolled their eyes in response. "Walk with me? I've a few questions to ask."

Teresa switched her mug into her other hand and then looped her arm around Hyde's. "Fire away."

"Not literally. I'm delicate," Hyde interjected.

"Did anything stand out about the spaghetti to you?" Fynn led the way back to the bookshop. They walked quickly, ducking under awnings to avoid the freezing sprinkling of rain. "A smell or taste?"

"It tasted delicious. Smelled normal." Hyde sipped from the mug. They used it to point back towards Al Dente. "There was so much happening. So many spices and perfumes and flowers. I wouldn't have been able to isolate anything out of the ordinary unless it was extreme. Nothing was rotten or sickly or bad."

"Teresa?" Fynn jotted a few notes in his notebook.

"Hyde's sniffer is far better than mine. I didn't taste the dish." Teresa considered it for a moment. "Do you still have the leftovers?"

"All handed off for testing. And no, I'm not letting either of you anywhere near it." Fynn glowered at them until they both nodded. "I should really be asking you questions separately."

"Are we suspects?" Hyde sighed with a hint of resignation.

"Don't be daft." Fynn shook his head at Hyde's question. "You are the person least likely to murder someone in the entire village—probably the entire country."

"I shoved your boss."

"He probably deserved it. And you didn't shove him onto a wooden stake. Listen, we all know that while I have a healthy respect for the job he does as chief inspector, he's personally a wee bit of a berk." Fynn shrugged indifferently. "Back to the questions. Did anyone say anything odd?"

"Define odd." Hyde adjusted their flat cap when the wind threatened to blow it away. "I heard something, though it might've been nothing at all."

"What?"

"The man who died and his wife. Rocco and… I don't remember her name." Hyde glanced over at Teresa, who shrugged. She hadn't paid that much attention to the introductions. "Was it Pia?"

"Gia," Fynn corrected.

"Right. Rocco and Gia. They were having an argument in the corner of the room. I think everyone else was distracted by Amalia and her father having words. I didn't hear most of what they said." Hyde stopped walking and closed their eyes. They seemed lost in memory for almost a full minute before opening them again. "She mentioned something along the lines of 'this is a bad idea.' And I believe he said, 'It's too late to turn back.'"

"Anything else?"

"Dinner was served, so everyone came together." Hyde turned to Teresa, who shrugged once again. She hadn't heard any of the conversation. "My ears are annoyingly sensitive. I doubt anyone else in the room would've picked up on what they said."

"I won't ask if Amalia was near the food." He paused when Hyde huffed in irritation at him. "We have to ask questions. The meal was prepared by her and Battista in their restaurant. They had the easiest and longest access to the dish. How did she seem before the dinner?"

"Where is Amalia?" Hyde asked.

Teresa was almost tempted to take a step back. She knew Hyde wouldn't take kindly to questions that were suspicious of Amalia. "She was stressed, as any of us would be when confronted by estranged family members. Also, their joining us at the dinner was a surprise. She hadn't expected them."

"Where is Amalia?" Hyde repeated.

"DI Filippov and Chief Inspector Pacheco are asking her questions." Fynn kept his voice gentle. He usually had a great rapport with Hyde. "I'm not the enemy."

"She didn't kill anyone."

"And I'm sure our questions will lead to that conclusion. We have to do our jobs, Hyde." Fynn gave their arm a squeeze. "Can you think of anything else?"

"Nothing," Hyde muttered stubbornly.

"Hyde?"

They lifted their head to glance at Fynn. "I don't remember anything else."

"And if you do?"

"I'll tell you." Hyde muttered a semi-polite "Goodbye" and then wandered across the street towards the post office.

Teresa tried not to laugh at the put-out look on Fynn's face. "You have the great misfortune of following Pacheco, who riled them up this morning. They're not upset at you. And honestly, I don't think either of us saw or heard anything to prove or disprove a case against Amalia. It's mostly our instincts telling us she's innocent. Oh, I have a thought."

"Hmm?"

"Why don't you try tarot or tea leaves? Maybe you'll find answers."

"Hilarious." Fynn rolled his eyes while she laughed. "You know my sight doesn't work on command."

Teresa noticed Hyde moving past Between the Leaves. *Where are they going?* She waved at Fynn.

"We'll give you a ring if we remember anything else."

Jogging across the lane, Teresa easily caught up with Hyde. They grabbed Teresa's hand and pulled her along with them. It took a moment for her to realise they were following someone.

"Hyde? Hyde. What are we doing?" Teresa murmured.

"It's Amalia's father. Endo? Enzo? Enzo. That was it." Hyde rubbed their hand across their face. "Why am I so dreadful with remembering names? He was watching us while we chatted with Fynn. I thought it was a coincidence, but why would he be standing still the whole time? He turned and walked away the second I finished talking."

"It could be a coincidence." Teresa didn't believe it was. "Why are we following him?"

"I don't know. It's what they do in thrillers. They follow the suspect." Hyde tugged on her hand and dragged her behind a wall. "He might've spotted us."

"Hyde." Teresa closed her eyes for a moment. She pressed against the wall and gave up on trying not to laugh when they peeked out. "It's daylight."

"People are far less observant than you think." Hyde did make an excellent point. "I've spent a lot of time watching the world. It helps you learn how to fit in—even if you can't quite manage it perfectly."

"Hyde." Teresa always found herself a little heartbroken for the young vampire who'd struggled to find themselves as the lone autistic in their family coven. "What stands out to you about Enzo Bassani?"

"He tried very hard not to be noticed by us while putting a great amount of effort into listening to the conversation. His anger at the restaurant was out of place. He kept…." Hyde fell silent. They rubbed their hand across their forehead. "My memory is a little fuzzy. There was something about him and Gia. As I was passing out, when they were standing by the body. But I can't remember."

"It'll come back to you." Teresa patted them on the shoulder. "Don't try to force it. Oh, he's heading towards the loch."

"We should follow." Hyde had darted back onto the pavement before Teresa could stop them. "Maybe he'll do something interesting."

Teresa stared up at the grey skies overhead. "It was going to be such a lovely week."

9

HYDE

Loch Bard, renamed a few centuries back, was an immense sea loch. It fed into the inner sound where the river entered the North Atlantic Ocean. Once upon a time, it had been called something else, but Myrddin's contributions to the village had led to the change.

Hyde followed from a distance as Enzo Bassani strode through Raven Park. He slipped behind the row of cottages running to the west, which would inevitably take him to the pier. There wasn't much else on that side of the village in the direction he appeared to be going.

They skirted around the village ritual space. Hyde spared a glance at the remnants of the last sacred fire. It had been a Samhain one done in honour of Florence's passing.

The park itself was a vast open space leading down to the loch. A variety of trees and other plants made a natural barrier along the edges. There was also a communal gardening plot off on the east side. It was mostly filled with various herbs used in spells and rituals.

The village druids, dryads, and witches had carefully cultivated the gardening plot. They had their own sections with some crossovers. With help from Callie, Emrys managed to protect the area from the elements—not even cold winter blasts could ruin the plants.

Callie Daniel was the oldest dryad in the village. She ran the small supermarket across from the greengrocer, run by one of the younger druids in South Myrddin, Luke Dietz. The two worked well together to keep from doubling up on produce.

"Hyde?"

"Hmm?" Hyde kept their voice low. They'd finally made their way across the park, through the thick woods, and up the hill to where they'd last seen Enzo. "What?"

"What are we doing?"

"I don't… know." Hyde didn't let it stop them. Teresa slipped her hand into theirs. "I just feel like we should follow him."

When they finally came onto the lane leading to

the small pier, they spotted him again. Enzo had walked around the edge of the small inlet. He'd used the narrow footpath that went around the coast, leading out of the village and towards the Myrddin lighthouse, which sat on the tiniest of islands off the coast.

A small sandbar and coral reef connected the island to the mainland, only crossable during low tide. The lighthouse had once been where Emrys lived. It was still carefully taken care of by the village druids, who maintained the light.

They followed Enzo from a distance, making sure to duck out of sight if he stopped. He disappeared into a thicket of wild cherry trees. Hyde didn't hesitate to go after him with Teresa still holding their hand.

"I see them." Teresa caught Hyde by the back of their coat, dragging them behind one of the larger trees. "Down by the edge of the water."

"Them?"

"Enzo and Gia."

Hyde immediately poked their head out. They eventually spotted the father and daughter-in-law standing on the rocky shore. The two appeared deep in conversation. "They don't seem happy. A lot of wild gesturing. They're loud enough that I can almost hear them."

Shushing Teresa when she started to speak, Hyde tilted their head. They tried to tune out the sound of the wind in the trees, the water, the birds, and everything else. It was almost possible to make out their voices underneath it all.

"He's asking her what she did." Hyde hissed in frustration when the wind picked up, rustling the leaves around them. "I swear he said it hadn't gone to plan. Or it didn't go to plan. Or… something about a plan."

"Maybe we can move closer?"

"Not without them spotting us." Hyde didn't see any cover for them to hide behind if they exited the thicket. It was open ground, albeit rocky and uneven. Nowhere for them to disappear if Gia or Enzo happened to glance in their direction. "*Balls.* They're turning around."

"They can't see us."

"We have to ask them questions." Hyde couldn't shake the feeling that one of the Bassanis had been involved in the murder, and it wasn't Amalia.

"I have an idea." Teresa slipped her hand back into Hyde's. She casually strode out of the trees, tilting her head towards them and laughing as though they'd said the funniest joke. "It's a lovely day for a walk."

"It isn't." Hyde peered up at the gradually darkening skies. It was definitely going to rain soon. They glanced sharply at Teresa when she poked them in the side. "What?"

"It's a lovely day for a walk." She said the words even louder this time, plastering a fake smile on her face when the Bassanis drew closer. "Good morning. Enjoying the sights of the village?"

"We are." Enzo didn't sound as though he was enjoying anything at all, particularly not their presence. "I'm surprised you're up and about."

"Me?" Hyde pointed to themselves. "Why?"

"Cursed food, remember?" Teresa muttered. She raised her voice when she focused back on Enzo. "Doctor thought fresh air would be good for them. How are you doing?"

"My son is dead. I am grieving." Enzo covered his face with his hands. He gave a long, shuddering breath before dropping them. His eyes glinted with something, though no tears fell. "I'm glad you weren't seriously injured by the dish. I never imagined Amalia's bitterness would extend so far. We assumed enough time had passed."

Hyde latched on to the last thing he'd said. "Enough time? Did she not know you were coming? She mentioned you received an invitation."

"No. We thought she might avoid us. Our family has been fractured long enough. I had hoped to bring

Amalia and Rocco together. They were close for so long. The fake invitation was his idea." Enzo brought his arm up to wrap around the silent Gia. She sniffled several times, swiping delicately at her eyes with a handkerchief. "It was obviously a mistake. He *obviously* poisoned her mind enough to turn her against her family."

Hyde narrowed her eyes. Enzo was likely referring to Battista. Amalia rarely spoke about her family, but she had done so enough for them to find the grieving father hard to believe. "You're so sure she did it."

"Who else? Battista? Not strong enough, and his powers run to a different bend. A family curse is always strongest against its own blood." Enzo glanced towards the still-silent Gia. "If you'll excuse us, I should get her back to our temporary accommodations. The police have asked us to remain in the village for a few days."

With a wave of goodbye, Enzo led his daughter-in-law down the path away from the water. Hyde watched them silently until they were out of sight. They tried to parse through the brief conversation. Something felt wrong.

"For all her dainty dabbing of her eyes, I didn't see one sodding tear." Teresa twisted around towards the water. "Let's see if they dropped something."

"Do you think he really believes Amalia did it?" Hyde strolled slowly behind Teresa, who inspected every inch of the ground. "I know I'm not the best at deciphering emotions, but his grief seemed real."

"It did." Teresa continued down to the edge of the water, clambering up one of the large rocks. "Gia was another story."

Nodding in agreement, Hyde meandered around the area. Nothing grabbed their attention. No random bit of paper or anything nefarious jumped out.

"There are ashes up here." Teresa crouched down on the large boulder. "Someone burned something. Paper, maybe? It's not a magic I recognise, but it doesn't feel inert."

Hyde climbed up to join her, kneeling for a better view. They bent over, getting as close as possible without shoving their nose in the ash. "We're lucky it's so damp this morning. Otherwise, I imagine it would've all floated away."

"What's your sniffer picking up?"

"It smells of burnt paper, mostly, or... no, *not* paper. Hair. Burnt hair. A hint of something else." Hyde didn't want to touch the drizzle-soaked ash. They worried about scattering it if the wind decided to pick up. "I've never been around either Amalia or

Battista when they're doing whatever it is incubi or succubi do. What do they do?"

"I've no idea."

"I've been too afraid to ask. Seems a little personal. Their magic is all their own. I know there's a whole subsection of romance novels dedicated to them. Though, from the way Amalia sneers at the covers, I don't think they're accurate." Hyde leaned in a little closer. "There's a faint musky scent underneath everything else."

Teresa fished her phone out of her pocket, taking a few photos of the small pile of ash. "We should tell Fynn what we've found."

Hyde visibly cringed when they remembered how curt they'd been to him. It hadn't been his fault. "I should apologise for being so ratty to him earlier."

"Hyde Snodgrass. Do not lick the ash." Teresa grabbed their arm when they bent even further down. "No."

Hyde sat back on their heels. "I wasn't."

"You were definitely thinking about it." Teresa poked them lightly with her phone. "I'm all for sniffing out the magic, but we can't go around licking all the evidence. It might have poison—and it gives Pacheco a reason to shout at us."

"He doesn't have to raise his voice. His facial expressions do the work for him."

"I'm now stuck with the visual of his eyebrows yelling at people." Teresa giggled. "I'm never going to be able to take him seriously ever again."

Hyde stared down at the ash. "Think we could take a sample for Battista to look at? Maybe he'd recognise the smell?"

Teresa looked up from where she'd been reading a message on her phone. "Fynn's on his way. He said not to touch anything."

"With our fingers?"

"He didn't specify." Teresa dug around in her pockets before pulling out a tiny glass jar. "It's clean. I was planning to harvest a few herbs from the communal garden."

"Not sure harvesting evidence is quite the same." Hyde inspected the ashes carefully before scooping up the tiniest amount. "It's not tampering with evidence, right?"

"Let's not get into the semantics of that conversation with Fynn or any of the other detectives." Teresa grabbed the jar. She leapt off the boulder and motioned for Hyde to join her. "I see him coming down the path."

As Hyde went to get to their feet, they spotted something they hadn't noticed. A sprig of a herb they couldn't identify. They scrambled for their phone, almost launching it out of their hands before finally managing to grab it.

"Hyde? Hurry up."

Hyde crouched down and snapped a few photos. They dropped down off the boulder, walking over to Teresa and showing them the image. "Have you ever seen this before?"

"Not sure. Where was it?" Teresa twisted around. She craned her neck, trying to see it. "How'd we miss that?"

"No idea. But I'm wondering if it's part of what they tried to burn. The rain is probably the only thing that saved any of the evidence." Hyde slipped their phone back into their pocket. They forced a smile when Fynn strode up to them. "Sorry, I was rude. It wasn't fair to take my mood out on you when Pacheco riled me up."

"He brings out the worst in people." Fynn graciously accepted the apology. "So, what've you found? And how did you find it?"

Exchanging a look with each other, Teresa finally took the lead. She gave an edited version of events, claiming they'd stumbled on Gia and Enzo in deep conversation. Fynn didn't seem to believe her entirely.

"Please don't put yourselves in danger again.

Promise me you'll be careful. Both of you." Fynn sighed when they both nodded. "All right, off with you. Let me collect the evidence before it disappears. And you two might as well get out of this miserable drizzle."

"Will you tell us if this turns out to be something?" Hyde asked.

"Is this because I encouraged your curiosity during Florence's case?" Fynn rubbed his forehead while smiling ruefully. "I won't give you the details because I can't. I will tell you if it's related or not. How's that?"

"Brilliant." Hyde waved cheerily at him.

Grabbing Teresa's hand, they rushed off before Fynn could change his mind. And they definitely didn't want him asking any questions. The storage jar would not be something they could easily explain.

They retraced their steps through the thicket of trees and the park. Teresa stopped walking as they made their way back onto Harbour Road. Hyde pulled their cap further down, grimacing as a drop of rain slipped down their neck.

"Why don't you see if Battista's home? I have to get the taco bus ready for the day." Teresa retrieved the jar from her pocket and handed it over. "If he doesn't know, maybe Emrys does? We can also ask the knitting group tonight. Someone has to have an idea of what we found."

"Perfect." Hyde darted in for a quick kiss before taking off at a jog. "Bye."

10

TERESA

After the brief kiss, Teresa watched Hyde race off towards Al Dente before veering off towards her vintage double-decker bus. It was going to be such a dreary day; it was tempting to keep shorter hours.

If the skies opened up any further, it would be a slow day. No one wanted to be out when rain poured down. She couldn't blame them.

The morning passed quickly. Teresa didn't prep as much as she normally would've. The weather forecast showed the rain unlikely to abate over the next twenty-four hours.

Teresa had a grand total of one customer for her lunch rush. She shook her head at a drenched Constable Trishna Jain. "Hello."

"Lovely day for it." Trishna ducked under the awning and breathed a sigh of relief. "All those water-repellent spells are absolutely worthless. They can't stand up to a solid Scottish rain."

"Hang on." Teresa dashed to the little storage closet built underneath the winding stairs of the bus. She grabbed a spare towel and an umbrella, handing both through the window to her fellow witch. "Dry yourself off. I'll fix up a load of tacos for you to share with your sister. I'm probably going to close up for the day."

"Anyone with any sense at all is indoors." Trishna shook her fist up at the sky. "Blasted rain."

"You did choose Scotland."

"I like to feel as if South Myrddin chose us." She dried herself off as best she could before carefully redoing the braid in her long black hair. "How are you both doing? How's our resident bookish vamp? Any leftover signs from the incident?"

"None that they've shared with me." Teresa worked quickly, fixing up a fair amount of what she'd made into tacos. She knew the constable would share with any of the police on duty. The food wouldn't go to waste. "How's the investigation going?"

"Above my paygrade." Trishna leaned in closer. "I will say they've finally released Amalia after questioning her for ages."

Teresa was relieved to hear that. It had been

concerning how long they'd held Amalia. She deftly finished up the last taco and sorted them into boxes before easing them into a bag. "Here. Hopefully, this will keep them from getting wet."

"You're a doll. Thanks." Trishna paid for the tacos and then waved, rushing off with her borrowed umbrella.

Teresa shook her head laughing when Hyde jogged past the constable. They waved at the bus before dashing into the bookshop. She peered up at the ever-darkening skies that had gotten impossibly greyer. "No one else is coming out in this weather."

It was already past lunch. The rush had been obviously non-existent. Teresa decided to call it a day.

With what was left over, Teresa made up a bunch of tacos for her own lunch to share with Hyde. She quickly cleaned up the kitchen and shut everything down. It didn't take long at all; she thought she could probably do it in her sleep at this point.

After a quick shower in the tiny bathroom upstairs and a change of clothes, Teresa raced the short distance between the bus and the bookshop. She headed inside, carefully shutting the door behind her. Hyde was behind the counter, messing with their signs.

"I've brought tacos."

"Excellent." Hyde nodded to the coffee table by the fire. "Go on. It's warmer over there. The cats are already making themselves cosy."

"Trishna said Amalia's been released. She couldn't tell me anything else." Teresa pulled the containers of food out of the bag, setting them on the table and carefully discouraging a curious cat paw or two from inspecting them. "Maybe they've realised she's not involved?"

"One can hope." Hyde brought over two glass bottles of black currant iced tea, a bookshop speciality that they only shared with a select few. "Battista took a look at the ashes and the photo of the bit of plant or herb I found."

"And?"

"He didn't smell or sense anything off them. Amalia wasn't there, so we can ask her." Hyde set the jar on the mantel above the fireplace, out of the way of the curious cats. "Maybe Emrys will swing by later. He might know something we don't.

"Think anyone's going to come to the Skeleton Crew this evening?" Teresa leaned over the table to take a bite of the taco. She deflected Pestle's reaching paw. "No mole for you."

"Mole. Mole. Mole. But not like mole, the animal." Hyde had always seemed to love the way the word sounded. They repeated it a few more times before taking a bite themselves. "Oh. These are delicious. Did you add something different? There's a tartness."

"Luke had a bunch of lovely radishes in at the greengrocer, so I decided to make my abuela's spicy pickled recipe for them. They're brilliant as thinly slivered toppings with the richer mole I used with the braised beef. And I fried the tortillas the tiniest bit more for the extra crunch." Teresa had experimented for a few days to get the combination right. "The creamy cheese along with the avocado. I'm really pleased with this recipe. I might put it on a more permanent rotation if I can keep getting the ingredients in."

"Delicious. You're a genius."

Teresa blushed. "I can't take credit for family recipes."

"Yes, you can. You've made them all your own." Hyde was stubborn in their disagreement. They inhaled the rest of their taco, careful not to lose any delicious morsels. "We know Amalia didn't do it, and neither did Battista."

"Correct."

"So, why would Enzo kill his son?" Hyde sipped their iced tea.

"Or Gia murder her husband?" Teresa bit into the last taco with some regret. She was definitely making this combination again. "But not just that, why do it at Amalia's restaurant? They'd been estranged from each other."

"I know we've had this conversation before… but it keeps rolling around in my head. If it was either Gia or Enzo, or both, they picked Al Dente on purpose. It wasn't an accident or a matter of a sudden opportunity. I imagine it would've been easier to do so on more familiar territory. Neither of them has ever been to South Myrddin. I've never seen them in my life." Hyde tapped their fingers against the glass bottle. "The only logical reason is that they wanted to frame Amalia."

"But why?" Teresa shifted so she was resting her back against the couch. "What do they gain if Amalia is put in jail? She'd still be alive."

"Maybe a way to punish her while getting rid of Rocco?" Hyde sounded as unsure as Teresa felt about the entire confusing mess. "We have to ask them questions."

"We? Them?"

"Yes, we. And I mean all of them. Amalia, Gia, and Enzo." Hyde had gone from unsure to stubbornly confident. Teresa sighed internally, having a feeling this would put them in conflict with Pacheco again. She had to admit, she was as curious as her partner. "I was almost collateral damage. I want to know why."

"Fair."

They finished up their tacos and tea in companionable silence. Mortar settled in for a nap by the fire while Pestle was content to chase the reflections of the twinkling lights around the room. He deftly avoided running into shelves with a practised ease.

Hyde gathered up the remnants of their late lunch and carried it over to the rubbish bin. "How about we do some research while we wait to see if the knitting circle is going to meet?"

"Okay." Teresa tried not to laugh when Hyde plucked up a massive stack of books that had been sitting on the counter. It was tall enough to reach the top of their head. "What's all this?"

"Every tome I have on incubi, succubi, and demons. There has to be something useful in here." Hyde paused when Mortar bumped against their leg. The beautiful Persian cat managed to lead them around the couch to where Teresa could grab half of the stack of books. "If nothing else, it gives us something to do while we wait."

With the coffee table cleared of food, they spread the books out between them. Hyde stoked the fire; the wind had picked up along with the rain, stripping away the heat. They settled together on cushions on the floor with their backs to the couch.

The bookshop was always such a comforting space. Teresa thought it perfectly matched its owner. Quirky with slightly crooked shelves filled with all manner of books. The magically created lights that ran along the top of the room. The hardwood floor with old threadbare rugs to dampen the sound. There were cushions and blankets in various corners for the cats.

And books.

Every book imaginable. Between the Leaves sometimes seemed more of a lending library than a proper shop. Hyde preferred to hunt for rare tomes while keeping a varied stock. It was as unique as the vampire who ran it—and perfect for the odd little village they inhabited.

"Where do we start?" Teresa was a little overwhelmed by the number of books spread across the table.

"Wiping our fingers?" Hyde held out a small flannel usually kept behind the counter for tea spills. They pulled out their phone and scrolled to the image of the tiny part of the plant they'd found. "Maybe we start with anything connected specifically to their creatures? It had to be, or I wouldn't have survived."

"So, we skim through for any plant references?" Teresa cleaned her fingertips and then set the flannel aside. "Probably the easiest to spot."

"There are even pictures," Hyde teased.

They worked in silence for a while. Mortar and Pestle made themselves comfortable in their laps. It was a companionable quiet, nothing but the turning of pages, crackling of the fire, and occasional purring from the cats. Teresa honestly thought she could spend the rest of her life like this—maybe without the side of murder.

11

HYDE

"Everything is starting to blur together." Teresa gently set the book down on the coffee table. "I'm not even sure any of those words made sense."

"It's in Greek."

"Then no, the words didn't make sense to me." Teresa opened it for a second time. "It is in Greek. Why do you have this?"

"I collect books on every magical being in the village. Creatures, witches, druids, demons, everything. I can read it." Hyde shrugged. They didn't often speak about all the languages they understood. It made them intensely uncomfortable. "I can feel you staring at me. Did I do something weird again?"

"Not weird. Brilliant." Teresa reached over to grab Hyde's chair, dragging them closer. She drew them in for a kiss. "You are absolutely brilliant, you know that?"

A tapping on the window interrupted their kissing. Mortar stretched languidly and sauntered over to the door. She leapt up, managing to turn the knob and open it.

With a buoyant caw, Odin guided Morrigan into the shop and over to her preferred chair in the knitting circle corner of the room. Hers was an old tufted velvet wingback in a faded teal. It had been hers from the start.

"Oh, Hyde. I've something for you. My great-niece in Mumbai sent me a special blend of masala chai." Morrigan hefted up her indigo cloth project bag. She dug through it before pulling out a beautifully decorated tin and tossing it in Hyde's direction. "You'll love it. It's well-balanced with a delicious combination of cinnamon, cardamom, and cloves, and it's a little heavy on the ginger. Ah. My sock. Odin? Have you unravelled this?"

With a caw of annoyance, Odin flew from her shoulder over to the mantel. He fluffed up before beginning to preen his feathers. The crow gave a shake, which sent little drops of water flying. Pestle hissed at the bird in annoyance.

"Play nicely, you two." Teresa went over to check

out Morrigan's latest project. "Think you've only lost a few stitches at most."

"That's probably Odin's way of complaining that he hasn't had any special treats recently. I know where you sleep, you feathered menace." Morrigan pointed one of her knitting needles in the general direction of the fireplace. She felt the partially completed sock with her fingertips. "Hmm. I think you're right. It shouldn't be too difficult to fix."

"Odin, you be nice to Morrigan," Hyde chided. They went over to the small tea station, digging around in the cabinet under the counter until they found the box of bird-friendly treats. "Here. Have this and do better."

Odin eyed them and the treat before gently snatching it with his beak. He ate messily before offering a caw of thanks. Hyde grinned brightly; they loved all the various animals around the village, always had.

Morrigan used a combination of her senses, magic, and her familiar bond with Odin to function in the world. "You're too kind to him."

"He's a beautiful boy. Any news on the letters?" Hyde had closed all the books, making sure to stick little cards to save their place. They gathered them up together and carried them over to the shop counter. "Did Emrys find anything?"

"Not yet. I spoke with him earlier. He's promised to continue testing them. No one's been harmed, and I'd prefer to keep it that way. We can't just assume whoever's sending them isn't going to figure out how to sneak one past me." Morrigan took her job of managing the village post quite seriously. "Amalia stormed by me earlier, didn't hear my hello. More grey clouds above her head than there were in the sky. I could feel the electricity and anger vibrating off her. Poor lass. Have you heard anything about the investigation?"

"We found this weird pile of ash." Teresa grabbed the bottle from the coffee table, carrying it over and taking the lid off. "We're not sure if it's connected, but there was something suspicious about it and who we found near it."

Taking the glass container, Morrigan lifted it up to her nose. She sniffed delicately before giving it a little shake. Odin flew over to sit on the back of her chair. He also inspected the ashes curiously.

"Not my brand of magic." Morrigan tilted her head towards Odin, who cawed low before tugging on her hair. She held the jar out to Teresa. "I'd ask Santi. I assume you're avoiding Amalia for the moment. Give her some time to calm down. But Santi's a demon—he might see something we don't."

Teresa sealed the jar and offered it to Hyde. "We will. I might have Emrys check it out."

"Poor Emrys. Always getting things shoved at him to sniff and inspect." Morrigan laughed loudly. Odin seemed to almost snicker with her. "That's what happens when you're ancient."

"Morrigan." Hyde knew the witch was deceptively older than most thought. She appeared to be in her thirties at most, but she'd been in the village when they'd arrived as a child. "If he's ancient…."

"Hyde Snodgrass. I taught you better than to comment on someone's age."

"You just called Emrys ancient." Hyde couldn't help grinning when Odin snickered again. "See. He agrees with me."

"He knows you'll give him treats." Morrigan deflected a poke from his beak easily. "Emrys is older than I, so I can call him ancient. And I have clearly moisturised more than he."

"Think more than moisturiser was required," Hyde muttered.

There were some witches and druids in the world who'd sacrificed an aspect of themselves or promised something. They'd always gain something in return. For some, they grew more powerful, and others never seemed to age.

The sacrifice could be great. Hyde had never

asked Morrigan about hers. It was an incredibly personal thing.

When Hyde had been a young vampire, Emrys had told them his story. Or he'd told them a very abbreviated version, at least. He'd promised to dedicate every aspect of his being to protecting the abandoned—his foundlings; he'd never aged beyond the day he'd done the ritual.

And he'd kept to his promise.

The foundlings in South Myrddin all found themselves under the protection of Emrys. Hyde had seen first-hand the lengths the druid would go. They'd always been grateful for the shelter found underneath his wings.

"Hyde?" Teresa tapped them on the arm. "Are you okay?"

"Yes, yes." Hyde nodded. They turned away from the others and went over to hunt for their current project. It was a chunky oversized cable knit jumper in an autumnal gradient. They'd already finished the lighter golden tones and had now moved to a deeper orange. A squeak from Pestle drew their attention. He was sitting by the shelf where they'd stashed the bag. "Ah. There it is. Thank you. Aren't you the most brilliant furry beast?"

"Please tell me you aren't talking about me, cub," Reuben rumbled from behind them.

"Well, you are furry, a beast, and consider your-self to be brilliant." Morrigan didn't even pause in her knitting. "They could be."

"Unless Reuben's wolf is a fluffy ginger cat, I wasn't talking about him." Hyde set their project bag on the counter. They hadn't expected to see the were-wolf. He usually kept a close eye on those in his boarding house. "Finished up the book I found you?"

"Not yet. Heard you had another run-in with the fanged menace. I wanted to make sure you were all right."

Hyde rolled their eyes. They moved further down the counter, crouching down to check the cupboards where they stored orders. It took a moment to find the right one. "Here. It arrived while you were away."

"I did come to check on you."

"Or you wanted to know if Inspector Berk survived his encounter." Hyde slid the book over the counter. "I'm fine. I was narkier than I should've been, but I can't take back the words now. Are you staying for the knitting?"

"No." Reuben snatched up his book. "I'll leave the clacking and yarn to others."

Hyde dodged his hand when he reached out to ruffle their hair. "Go on. Go howl at the moon or something."

"Take care of yourself, cub." He tucked the book inside his jacket to keep it dry and raced out of the shop into the gloomy weather.

Despite the rain and chill, the entire crew eventually arrived. Hyde made sure to have the kettle on for tea. The fire crackled merrily, and blankets were brought from upstairs just in case.

In no time at all, the group of eight were happily chatting away and working on various projects, from socks to embroidery to a chunky jumper. Hyde poured tea for everyone before settling down in their chair to start.

Pulling out their knitting needles, Hyde carefully inspected them to make sure they hadn't gotten damaged. They were the most unique out of the group. A set made from scrimshaw that had been gifted to them by Florence.

It was also what had given the knitting circle its moniker. The scrimshaw needle set wasn't exactly a full skeleton, but it had been enough of one to give Hyde the idea. They loved the name.

"Now." Winifred leaned forward in her chair. She held her cup of tea out to Flossie, who poured a dram of liquor from a battered silver flask. No one ever asked what was in it. "What's this about Amalia murdering her brother?"

All the knitting and crocheting needles froze

briefly. Every eye turned in Hyde's direction. Mortar hissed, causing all of them to return to their projects.

Hyde let out the breath they'd been holding from the anxiety of so much intense attention. They ran their fingers lightly over Mortar's head in thanks. "Not sure I have anything new or earth-shattering to share. You've all heard everything already. We were going to have dinner at Al Dente. Something was done to one of the dishes—and the brother died."

"And you were sick," Teresa added.

"Not on purpose." Hyde hesitated before grabbing the jar of borrowed evidence. "We found this on a rock near the shore. I don't have a clue what it is, but I can't shake the sense that there's something to it."

"Here." Santi carefully set the lace shawl he was making for Morrigan to one side. He stretched an arm out to take the glass container. "Definitely ashes."

"Yes, thank you, love. How about sharing something not obvious?" Morrigan teased him.

Hyde was happy that all eyes had been drawn elsewhere. Morrigan, Santi, and Rees had kept their relationship fairly under wraps until recently. It was always lovely to see their friends happy.

"Patience is a virtue." Santi ignored the looks far more easily than Hyde could've. He unstoppered the jar, bringing it up for a sniff. "I'd expect this to smell more strongly of fire."

Hyde shifted forward in their chair. "Yes. There's a whiff, but for a pile of sodden ashes, it's far too faint."

"Not an ordinary substance or fire, then." Santi turned his hand and dumped the contents onto his palm. He set the jar aside. "Hyde?"

"Yes?"

"Do you still have some of the ritual paper I gave you?" Santi touched some of the ash, spreading it out. He tapped a finger into it and delicately touched it to the tip of his tongue. "Definitely not an ordinary fire."

"Ha!" Hyde gestured toward Santi before turning to Teresa, who had covered her face with her hands. "See? See. It's a completely valid method of using your senses."

Teresa groaned into her hands. She finally lifted her head to glower at Santi. "Really?"

"I'm a demon. If it's what I believe it is, it won't harm me." Santi looked bewildered by the strong glare being sent in his direction. "Why are you acting as though I've insulted you and your ancestors?"

Hyde broke into giggles. They leaned against the counter where they'd been hunting for the ritual paper. "Resa—"

"Don't even start. You are not a demon." Teresa still laughed along with Hyde. She frowned when Santi seemed to suddenly focus his attention on the ashes. "What is it?"

"You found this in the village?"

"On one of the larger rocks to the north of the docks." Hyde pulled themselves together to answer. They finally spotted the wooden chest with the papers. "Why?"

"Have you shared this with the police?" Santi ignored their question.

"Yes."

"I'd wager my life that this was the anchor to a ritual. And not a good one." Santi dumped most of the ashes back into the jar and saved the rest in his hand. "You found the paper?"

Hyde carried a scrap of parchment over to him. They watched him tilt his hand and gingerly dump the ash onto it. "What the—"

The instant the ash touched the paper, it began to smoke. Santi murmured under his breath. Hyde thought it was ancient Greek. They could understand a word or two.

Santi finally folded the paper around the ash, tucking the packet into his pocket. "Someone anchored their curse to the object that they then burned to destroy their ritual. It's subtle. Not one I've encountered before. They're definitely in my realm of being."

"A demon?"

"Of some variety." Santi shrugged. "I'll give this to Fynn. He'll want to know."

"Santi...." Hyde glanced over at Teresa.

"I won't say how I found it." Santi grinned. "He'll know I'm lying, but he won't tell the big bad Pacheco."

12

TERESA

The knitting group went long into the night, as always. Laughter, gossip, and tea spiked with whatever tipple Flossie and Winifred had brought. Teresa helped Hyde clean up, then trudged the short distance from the bookshop to her bus. She barely managed to change before collapsing into bed, exhausted.

It had been a long few days. Teresa hadn't fully processed the fear of Hyde passing out in front of her. She'd been so petrified of losing them.

It's fine.

Hyde's fine.

It was a mantra Teresa repeated to herself while counting her breaths until anxiety stopped clawing at her. Some days, it was like a living being. She tried to

settle her nerves and not obsessively focus on what might've been.

A loud caw outside her window woke her up out of a deep sleep. Teresa forced her eyes open. She turned her head to find Odin pecking at the glass.

"Shite." Teresa tried to calm her racing heart. "What are you doing, you sodding feathered menace?"

The cawing and pecking continued. Teresa quickly climbed out of bed and threw on some clothes. She assumed something had happened to Morrigan. Why else would her familiar be at the bus?

But then Teresa smelled smoke. She bolted down the stairs, tripping and almost going headfirst through one of the windows. She righted herself and continued outside.

"Oh my goddess. Hyde," Teresa screamed. "Hyde!"

There was a line of fire in front of Between the Leaves. A glowing river of orange and red that was so bright, it hurt her eyes. It flowed from the door in either direction as if hunting for a way inside the building.

Rushing back onto the bus, Teresa filled her largest pot with water. She dashed out and threw it at what appeared to be the source of the fire.

Nothing happened.

Teresa cursed under her breath in English and Spanish. She dropped the pot and raced back inside, hunting for her fire extinguisher, praying to every god and goddess that it would work. "C'mon, c'mon."

As Teresa finally found it in one of the cabinets, she heard a loud, jarring chime ring through the village. Part of the warning system built into the protections around South Myrddin. She didn't breathe a sigh of relief just yet, but at least help would be coming.

Teresa lifted the fire extinguisher and paused. "What…?"

The fire hadn't spread to the building. It was as though it had hit an invisible wall. No matter how far it went, either vertically or horizontally, the flames couldn't touch the shop.

Help arrived as Teresa tried fruitlessly to put out the flames. Nothing seemed to stop them. Emrys showed up with Santi, Battista, and Amalia close behind. She could hear sirens in the distance. Other villagers rushed up to join them.

Emrys motioned for Teresa to lower the fire extinguisher. "That won't help."

"Hyde's still inside."

"Then they are safe." Emrys had brought his staff, an old, weathered branch of burnt wood. Something he rarely used. He murmured fiercely while gesturing violently towards the flames. "There's no need to be alarmed."

Despite wanting to disagree quite loudly, Teresa held her tongue. Emrys raised his voice and stepped towards the flame. They rose up higher, seeming almost angry at his intervention.

Ill intent rolled off the flickering flames. The fire puffed up before disappearing in a whisper of acrid smoke. Nothing remained aside from a pile of ash and burnt branches by the front door, which had obviously been the source of ignition.

"Should we wait for the police? It's evidence." Teresa wanted to rush inside but didn't want to disturb the scene.

Santi crouched by the pile. He dipped a finger into the ash, unaffected by the heat still lingering. He glanced briefly at Teresa, then walked over to Emrys. She inched closer to listen. "It's the same as the ash they found by the water yesterday."

"Is it, now?" Emrys narrowed his eyes. He caught sight of Constable Vitya Antonov approaching, obviously the village police on duty that evening. "You'll want to contact one of your detectives. Someone's tried to burn one of my foundlings alive."

"Emrys." Vitya held his hands out, trying to placate the enraged druid. "We have no idea who set the fire or if it's connected to anything else. We shouldn't jump to conclusions."

"You shouldn't jump to anything." Emrys spoke softly, but his voice trembled with raw power. Teresa couldn't recall ever seeing him fully demonstrate his capabilities in the past—he seemed to barely have control over himself. "Call your detectives if they want to collect the evidence."

"Can I come out now?"

Teresa tilted her head back and saw Hyde's poking out from one of the upper windows. "Front door is blocked."

"I'll go out the back, then." Hyde vanished, shutting the window behind them.

"See? They're fine." Vitya was still attempting to soothe everyone's anger while also calling in the fire. He paused to speak on the phone before returning to talking with Emrys. "This is now a crime scene."

"Obviously." Amalia stepped into the conversation. "You may want to speak with my sister-in-law. Fire is one of her specialities."

Teresa perked up at that snippet of information. She wanted to press for more, but Hyde came careening around the corner with a cat in their arms and another draped across their shoulders. It took immense willpower not to break into giggles. "You didn't think to change?"

"Why?" Hyde glanced down at their blue flannel pyjama bottoms, duck T-shirt, and fluffy duck slippers. They'd clearly stopped to throw a thick robe on. "It's the middle of the night. I was in bed before all this racket."

"This racket?" Vitya rubbed his forehead. "Someone tried to set your bookshop on fire."

"Yes, but Emrys put protections on it ages ago when I first opened." Hyde wandered over to inspect the front door. "Not even a speck of soot on the stained glass. I'm fine."

"Someone tried to kill you."

"They're not very good at it." Hyde glanced between Teresa and Emrys, who had both sighed in exasperation almost in unison. "What? Am I wrong?"

"Don't tempt them to try harder. Please?" Teresa walked over to join them, looping her arm around Hyde's back and drawing them away from the source of the fire. "I was absolutely terrified when I saw a wall of flames in front of your shop."

"Yes, but I knew I was safe." Hyde drew their robe around them and tied the belt. They adjusted Pestle in their arms. "I was having such a strange dream as well."

"Hyde." Teresa forced herself to take a few deep breaths. They had very different perspectives on the incident. Hyde had been safely in the shop, knowing it was protected, while she'd been outside staring at a mountain of flame. "Someone tried to kill you. Twice."

"Not sure we can count the first time. They weren't aiming for me. At least, I don't think they were." Hyde smiled when Mortar rubbed her head against them. "I've no doubts it was absolutely terrifying from the outside. Not much I can do about it now, though."

Hyde's practicality could be as amusing as it was frustrating at times. They weren't intentionally making light of the situation. Their mind simply processed things differently.

Deciding to let it go, Teresa rested her head against Hyde's shoulder. It was easier to breathe with them safely outside the bookshop, even if there had never been any real danger.

From Teresa's perspective, the fear had been justified. She'd never seen fire behave the way this had. It had danced and flowed with a life of its own.

Not like the bright and cheerful ritual fires in the park. This had been dark and menacing. It was as if the one who conjured it had infused their own emotions into their creation.

With the excitement over and the emergency services arriving, the crowd began to disperse for the most part. A few villagers lingered. Teresa remained glued to Hyde, not wanting to let them out of her sight just yet.

Detective Inspector Filippov arrived not long after the constables. Nastia Filippov was a vampire. A stylish blonde who'd moved to the Highlands from Sofia in Bulgaria almost forty years earlier. She was particularly close with the Scottish coven and DCI Pacheco.

Hyde tensed when DI Filippov stepped towards them. "Where's Fynn?"

"DI Baines has the night off. You're stuck with me." Her tone seemed to say, *"Deal with it."* "What happened?"

"A fire." Hyde sank their fingers into Mortar's silky grey fur. "I didn't even see it until they began making a commotion. You'll have to talk to Teresa or anyone else who saw the flames first-hand."

"It was at your bookshop."

"And I was asleep." Hyde leaned into Teresa when she tightened her arm around their back. "Emrys put a protection around the bookshop. I didn't hear or smell anything at all. No aspect of the fire penetrated the building."

DI Filippov gave a sharp nod before turning icy blue eyes in Teresa's direction. "And you?"

"Odin woke me up, cawing and pecking at the window of the bus. I smelled smoke and came rushing outside to find the fire in front of Between the Leaves." Teresa definitely didn't have the same almost untouched practicality as Hyde. It had shaken her to see the danger licking so closely to the building. "I tried water and then a fire extinguisher. Nothing seemed to diminish the flames. It felt… angry."

"What felt angry?" Emrys stepped closer to her, ignoring the aggravated huff from the detective. "The fire?"

Teresa glanced between the two before nodding. "It was intense. I've never felt emotions from a fire before. It was malevolent. I don't know who did this, but they meant to cause harm, even if they were unsuccessful."

"Interesting." DI Filippov jotted a few notes into her notebook. She looked between the three of them and then at the cats, who hissed almost in unison. "Settle down, beasts. I don't mean your vampire any harm. Can you tell me anything else about the fire?"

"Santi Belrose mentioned the ashes were similar to the ones found out by the water," Emrys answered for the three of them. "I believe DI Baines took a sample."

Filippov's eyes narrowed on them. "And how would Santi know?"

"I...." Hyde trailed off when all eyes swung in their direction. "I have no idea. Magic."

"We'll leave that part out when I speak with the DCI. He's going to want to know about this fire." She took a single step closer to Hyde. "No matter how he fumbles his approach, he cares about the safety of all vampires."

"Safety, yes. Perhaps not so much their emotional and mental wellbeing or their overall happiness." Hyde pressed their lips together, seeming to regret the response. They cuddled Mortar more tightly to their chest. "Can I go inside now?"

"As long as you use the back door. The fire doesn't seem to have affected the building at all, and all the evidence is by the front door. I'll let you know once we've collected everything and it's usable again." DI Filippov motioned for all of them to move back. She frowned when Emrys didn't budge at all. "You are not involved in the investigation."

"Watch me."

Teresa pulled Hyde away from the detective and the druid. "We'll let them do whatever it is they're about to do."

"Have a massive row in the middle of the street." Hyde led the way around the bookshop to the back door. They could hear the start of the argument behind them. "Maybe if we're lucky, they'll distract Pacheco enough that he won't want to talk to me."

"I'll keep my fingers crossed," Teresa said.

"That might get annoying after a while." Hyde pushed open the door and let the cats leap off them. They immediately went to one of their favourite piles of blankets. "Not sure you can do a lot of cooking with your fingers crossed."

"Figuratively crossed, not literally."

13

HYDE

TERESA HAD CLEARLY BEEN MORE SHAKEN UP BY THE fire. Hyde tried to look at it from her perspective. It was hard for them to push their mind to process it.

For them, they knew they were fine. The fire wasn't going to do any harm other than be an annoyance. It was easy to be almost blasé about the attack when they'd known they weren't in any real danger.

Hyde thought about seeing the taco bus on fire. They imagined a wall of flame between them and Teresa. It sent a shiver of absolute terror through them. "I'm sorry."

"For?" Teresa stood up from where she'd been inspecting one of the bookshelves. "Hyde? What's wrong?"

"You were scared."

Teresa blinked a few times, tilting her head to the side. "I... was."

"You were scared for me because of the fire." Hyde tried to sort through the overwhelming number of thoughts swirling through their mind. "I didn't understand. I knew I was fine, but you had no way to know."

"Right."

Hyde rubbed their face a few times. "I'm not explaining this well."

"Take your time."

"I wasn't worried, so I didn't understand why you were worried. But if I had run outside to find your bus on fire, I would've been absolutely petrified." Hyde stepped around the cats who'd come over to check on them, clearly sensing their distress. "I didn't intend to be dismissive, but I was. I'm sorry."

Teresa drew Hyde into a hug. They stood in the bookshop with the cats winding between their legs for several minutes. "I'm glad you're okay. It felt like all the lies my anxiety told me were true. Everything was going to end badly. End wrong. The worst was going to happen."

Hyde slipped their arms around Teresa, tightening them cautiously to avoid their full strength.

"But it didn't. I'm okay. Just as weird as I was the day before."

"I'm glad you're okay."

"Me too." Hyde breathed a sigh of relief, happy to have some of the confusion cleared up. They never liked leaving things to fester; it only made matters worse. Something occurred to them as they lingered in Teresa's arms. "Santi said the ashes reminded him of what we found earlier."

"I heard."

"That means one of the Bassanis was involved. What if…?"

"Not Amalia," Teresa added when Hyde trailed off, lost in thought. "We know she wouldn't hurt you, either with a curse, poison, or setting fire to the bookshop."

Hyde pulled away from Teresa. They wandered back to where they'd left the stack of books. "One of these focused on demons who had an affinity to fire. Maybe we'll find something useful."

They paused, setting one of the books aside and moving to the lockbox behind the counter. They retrieved their family grimoire. It might contain notes about demons.

Handing one of the books to Teresa, the two cuddled together on the sofa. Hyde had mixed emotions about the Snodgrass Journal. They traced their fingers down the ribbed spine and over the family sigil at the bottom.

On the front cover, the sigil was embossed in leather. Her family crest of a martlet floating above a globe with various symbols inside the circle. The swallow-like bird without feet was done in silver. Hyde had never quite understood the meaning of it. And no one had ever taken the time to explain it to them.

Resting their hand on the cover, Hyde allowed the family magic to wash over them. It tingled along their fingers. Their nose twitched with the urge to sneeze.

"Are you okay?" Teresa rested a comforting hand on their knee. "We can do this later."

"I'm fine. I can't spend my entire life avoiding this. It's a journal. Grimoire. History. All the above. I can detach myself from personal connection." Hyde tried to sound confident, though they weren't sure. "I can."

"I don't think you can. No matter what happened in the past, they're your family. Maybe you don't claim each other, but I'm not sure blood and magic care." Teresa had personal experience, as did many in the village, with the complicated nature of familial relationships. "You don't have to throw away every-thing—at least not your history."

"Maybe."

The pages almost sang when their fingers skimmed over them. They flipped through the grimoire, hunting for anything about demons while pondering over Teresa's words. It was three-quarters through the journal when they found a small paragraph about demonic flame.

"Interesting."

"Find something?" Teresa set the book in her hands down and shifted closer to Hyde.

"Listen to this. Demonic Fire is controllable. It carries the wielder's intent within its embers. Each branch of creature—their words, not mine—is imbued with a variant all their own. It can be deadlier than any other conjured flame." Hyde finished reading. They traced the slope of the letters that flowed across the parchment. The handwriting was beautiful and precise. "They've repeated themselves with unnecessarily flowery words. My ancestors were pretentious."

"A different time when fancy words and handwriting were in fashion."

"Nothing on incubi or succubi specifically or any other demon. What's the point of mentioning variants if you aren't going into detail?" Hyde grumbled. They continued to skim through the next few pages. "I don't need an ancient Snodgrass text to tell me 'fire bad.' I grasped the concept as a toddler."

A knock on the front door interrupted their research. Pestle was out of the blankets and striding over to the door before Hyde had even stood up. He managed to get the door open, allowing Pacheco, Filippov, and Emrys to file into the shop. The latter didn't look pleased by the police presence.

Hyde groaned loudly at the sight of them, glaring at Teresa when she snickered. "Was I not supposed to make the sound out loud?"

"No, no, we usually don't groan in disgust when we see people quite so vocally." Emrys seemed as bemused as Teresa.

Hyde decided to ignore both of them, focusing on Pacheco. "I was very specific about your presence in my shop."

"Someone tried to kill you." Pacheco took a step forward, brushing Emrys's hand away when the druid went to grab his shoulder. "I thought we could clear the air."

"Air is cleared. Not a sign of smoke."

"Figuratively," Teresa muttered.

"Ah. Yes. Hmm." Hyde didn't like all the attention pointed in their direction. They were tempted to switch the sign over to Shh. "I had my say. I suppose it's only fair."

"I make mistakes." Pacheco ignored the snort from Emrys. "I am the lone vampire with the weight of an entire coven on my shoulders, not to mention the police force. I have done my best—but that has clearly been insufficient."

"You ignored suffering."

"Emrys. That's not helping." Hyde held a hand up, hoping he'd calm himself down. They'd had enough drama for one day. Their attention returned to Pacheco, who seemed to be waiting for them to say something. "I don't know how I'm supposed to respond. You're merely stating the obvious."

"I cannot intervene in every family matter."

"I cannot intervene in every family matter," Hyde mimicked in a mocking tone. They scrubbed their hands over their face tiredly. "You can't have it both ways. Are you a coven leader or not? Do you protect those under your fangs? That sounds wrong. Under your wings? You don't have them. Actually, I am tired of this conversation. I don't want to have it anymore. It's done. Maybe you can stop being such an absolute—"

"Hyde." Teresa caught the back of their robe, giving it a gentle tug. "Breathe."

"Do I theoretically need to breathe? I mean, they classify us as undead. But we're born. Like, actually and literally born."

"Not the time." Teresa snickered quietly. "I'm more than willing to have the debate over more tacos and wine, but maybe not now?"

"Right. The fire. Death. A murder. More important than philosophically debating whether I'm undead." Hyde scratched their head for a moment, ruffling their curls. "What was I saying? Ah, yes. You're a berk. Please stop pretending you have our best interests at heart when your solution is to do nothing. If you're going to be a coven leader, do so by starting with protecting the children. All the young vampires you are failing. Start there. Do something for them. I don't need your help now. I found a path for myself with the help of my family here in South Myrddin."

"I will."

"Good." Hyde walked over to the sign on the shelf. They flipped the Hello to Shh, then eyed the They before flipping it to She. "I am going over there."

"Hyde dropped her metaphorical microphone." Teresa stepped between her and the police. "How about I answer whatever questions you have?"

14

TERESA

In the awkward silence that followed, Hyde seemed completely oblivious. She meandered over to her favourite armchair by the fire, started the flames going, and cuddled up with the cats. Mortar sat up on her shoulder and kept a wary eye on the intruders.

Teresa decided the cats had Hyde well in hand, so she turned her attention to the detectives and druid. "You had questions?"

Pacheco had been silent the entire time. He, for all his faults, wasn't a fool. She knew he was one of the most powerful vampires in Europe and incredibly intelligent, just one who happened to have a massive blind spot when it came to Hyde.

"You mentioned the crow woke you."

"Odin. Morrigan's familiar. I heard tapping, and

then he cawed loudly. He can be annoyingly persistent when he wants to be. Never been more grateful to the bird in my life." Teresa knew now that Hyde hadn't been in danger, but her anxiety kept pinging at her brain. She could've lost her. One change of fate might've cost her so much. "I smelled the fire first and rushed out of the bus. It...."

"Teresa?" Emrys prompted when she stared blankly towards the stained-glass windows. "It what?"

"I remember thinking the fire moved like water. It met the boundary of Emrys's protection and then flowed out and up, hunting for any crack in the wall. A living, breathing flame." Teresa closed her eyes. She could almost feel the heat even now, despite it being gone. "Is it possible for a demon to control their flame from a distance? Or, once set, is it a separate entity? The hatred off it was tangible."

"I'll ask Amalia. She'd know the abilities of those in her family best." Emrys raised an eyebrow when both of the police detectives glowered at him. "Yes?"

"We will ask Amalia," Pacheco stated firmly, as if his words were an end to the matter. His gaze darted over to Hyde and back to Teresa. "Let us know when she's ready to converse."

Teresa bit her tongue to keep from saying "never" and simply nodded. The police stepped out of the shop, shutting the door behind them. She wilted into the nearest chair with a groan—all the adrenaline sustaining her had vanished. "Amalia...."

"Amalia Bassani is a clever demon. She won't allow the police to tie her up. Let someone else worry about the mess her family made. You take care of each other, and maybe keep out of this one? For the sake of my nerves." Emrys winked at her. He went over to Hyde, bending down to mutter quietly to her before standing up and heading towards the exit as well. "Rest well, foundlings."

The sound of the crackling fireplace in the bookshop usually relaxed Teresa. She could almost stand to be in front of it now. The flickering light was mesmerising, though they were both eventually lulled into a restless sleep, weighed down by the chaotic events of the early-morning hours.

Banging on the door jolted both of them awake. The hearth was filled with glowing embers but nothing more. Mortar and Pestle were stretched out languidly in front of it, soaking up the last bits of warmth.

Hyde groaned when the knocking continued. "How long did we even sleep?"

"A few hours? Maybe." Teresa groaned in pain when she stretched. "This armchair was not meant for napping."

"Maybe for the cats." Hyde stumbled out of the blanket, struggling to get unwrapped. She hopped a few times until she freed herself. "I'm coming. Stop knocking before you wake the dead."

"Hyde."

Teresa got up as well when she heard the panic in Rosa's voice. "So much for a calm morning."

Rosa rushed into the bookshop the second the door was opened. "They've arrested Amalia. Or detained her. Or taken her for questioning."

"What?" Hyde exchanged a bewildered look with Teresa. "For what?"

"I don't know. I saw Nastia leading her away. Battista thinks they found evidence they believe connects her to the murder, but they wouldn't tell him anything else." Rosa kept her voice low, as though expecting her uncle to pop up behind her. "I spoke with a friend in Duirnish. Their wee library has a book on incubi and succubi specifically. I thought perhaps it might offer answers."

While Hyde appeared to still be processing the news about Amalia, Teresa considered their options. She had to get Guac-A-Mole ready for the day. But the bookshop didn't necessarily have to open, particularly after the fire.

"How about you two go to the library and check out those books? I'll keep an eye on the shop while

I'm getting the taco bus ready for the day. I can't afford too many quiet days like yesterday." Teresa grunted when Hyde threw her arms tightly around her. "Careful. We don't all have vampire-proof ribs."

Hyde gave her another squeeze before releasing her. She switched the Shh sign back to Talk. "You'll be careful."

"I'll be fine. Go see if there's anything about demonic flames and curses." Teresa drew her in for a quick kiss. They both ignored Rosa's whistle behind them. "I'll make sure Mortar and Pestle don't get into too much trouble."

"Give me five seconds to be in something other than pyjamas and fluffy slippers." Hyde darted up the stairs into her flat above the shop.

"Don't worry. I'll take good care of her." Rosa leaned against the counter. "I don't understand why they've arrested Amalia. What would her motivation be in attacking Hyde?"

"Maybe they're convinced Hyde was collateral damage for the cursed pasta, and the fire was to stop us investigating?" Teresa didn't believe it for a moment, but she could see how a police investigation might have led down that path. "Just a thought."

"My uncle refuses to listen to me. I called him. He said he couldn't discuss it and that it was an ongoing investigation. They're 'following the evidence.'" Rosa sighed derisively. "He wouldn't even tell me if she'd been arrested officially."

"Can you be unofficially arrested?" Teresa went over to make sure Mortar and Pestle had food and water. They could open the door to head into the flat, so she wasn't too worried about them.

"She has a solicitor, right?"

"Battista called them for her."

Teresa met Rosa's worried gaze. "It'll all work out, won't it?"

"I have problems with my uncle, but he's a good detective. He believes in finding justice and truth." Rosa patted Teresa's hand. "Let's just hope whoever did this made a mistake."

15

HYDE

THE DRIVE TO DUIRNISH WASN'T A LONG WAY. THEY'D gone the scenic route by one of the smaller highland lochs. Rosa had put in one of her punk rock playlists. They sang along loudly and mostly out of tune to Defanged Menace—one of their favourite vampire bands.

"What the—" Rosa shouted as her little Mini Cooper suddenly swerved violently from one side of the lane into a stone wall and then careened off the lane. They flew the short distance down the embankment, hitting a dip that launched the car into the air. "Bloody hell, Hyde. Hold on."

Holding on was all they could manage when the vehicle crashed into the loch. They'd landed a decent way from shore and were sinking fast. Hyde scrambled to get free from her seat, already feeling like they were far too deep underwater.

"Oh. Bugger." Rosa lifted the broken pendant from around her neck. "Prepare yourself for the most annoying brand of assistance known to vampire kind."

"What?"

"Family magic. This being broken alerts my uncle that I'm in trouble. Don't ask how it works. I've never been able to figure it out. Some ancient, like older than him, secret. It's in our grimoire, which I am loath to touch." Rosa shook her head. "We have more pressing problems than Uncle Jonatan. We have to get out of here."

"Okay. Okay."

"Let's not panic. We're vampires. We don't die easily." Rosa quickly unbuckled her seat belt. She reached over to help Hyde, who'd been yanking repeatedly on hers and definitely panicking. "We're going to be fine."

"We're sinking. How deep is the loch?" Hyde grabbed for the door but was unable to get it open. "We have to break the glass and swim out. Isn't that what they do in movies?"

"I have no idea how deep this loch is. We're not completely submerged." Rosa shifted, trying to get the right angle to kick the windscreen. "Sodding steering wheel is in the way. Hyde? I need you to breathe and focus—then see if you can break the window."

"Right. Okay. Right. Right."

Muttering to herself under her breath, Hyde attempted to kick through the windscreen. Her first attempt failed epically. Her shoes didn't connect hard enough to so much as cause a dent.

The water was definitely rising around the vehicle. They had to get out. Being a vampire wasn't a definite assurance of immortality.

"You can do this. Take a breath. Focus," Rosa encouraged.

It took three kicks before the heel of her shoe hit the windscreen, splintering it like a slowly growing spider's web. Her fourth hit broke it entirely. Water instantly rushed inside.

Rosa grabbed her hand, keeping her from immediately panicking. She dragged Hyde forward through the broken window. They quickly breached the surface, and cold air hit their faces. "We're okay. Hyde? We're okay."

The Mini Cooper had flown an impressive distance into the loch. They were halfway back to shore when DCI Pacheco arrived. He dove into the water, not bothering to kick off his shoes or take off his jacket, quickly approaching them.

"This wasn't our fault," Hyde muttered.

"Mx Snodgrass—no, Hyde. I don't care about the whos and whys right now. Are you hurt? Were either of you injured? Rosa?" Pacheco dragged both of them to the shore. He crouched beside them once they were safely sat on the ground. His expensive suit was wrecked by the murky water. "I've called an ambulance. I happened to be close by when I felt the charm break."

"I'm not hurt." Hyde had begun to shiver violently from the shock, not from cold. "Just… shaky."

"I'm fine. Not a scratch on me. Though I could do without being soaked to the bone or covered in muck." Rosa plucked a stray plant out of her hair. "I don't know what happened."

"You lost control."

"Yes… and no." Rosa twisted around to point up towards the lane. "It was as though I'd hit a patch of ice, which is impossible. Not cold enough. But all the traction was gone. Something was strange about it."

"Chief Inspector?" Hamish's voice carried down to them. "Can they walk, or will they need help?"

"I can walk." Hyde got to her feet. She stumbled like a shaky newborn calf up the embankment to where Hamish waited.

He wrapped his arm around her, guiding her

towards the waiting ambulance. "Is this you being more careful?"

"I was a passenger. I claim no ownership in being launched into the blasted loch," Hyde grumbled. She grimaced at how sodden her cardigan had become. "Wool can withstand a lot—not sure drowning in murky Scottish water counts."

"Have you got a shirt underneath?" Hamish got her seated in the ambulance and rummaged around in one of the cabinets. He glanced over his shoulder, waiting for her to nod. "All right. Pop off the cardigan, and we'll get a blanket for you."

"I can't stop shivering."

"Vampires don't get cold. They aren't affected by the temperature." Hamish wrapped the emergency foil blanket around her. "You're in shock."

"I'm defective." Hyde shrugged. "Am I going to be roasted in the oven? Feels like I am."

"Not that kind of foil, Hyde. Well, not technically." Hamish crouched in front of her. "You're not defective. You're unique."

"Unique is the polite way of saying defective." Hyde gripped the blanket tightly. Her fingers dug through the foil wrap. "Are you sure this isn't the same sort used in cooking? I swear I've seen rolls in the kitchen at Al Dente."

"Hyde." Hamish quickly checked her vitals. "You are, I'm afraid, still undead."

"Technically, not undead. I mean, who defines what undead means? You can obviously tell I'm alive." Hyde pressed her lips together to keep from rambling further. Stress and anxiety often manifested in one of two ways—say nothing or say all the things. "Is Rosa okay?"

"She appears to be in deep debate with her uncle over her driving abilities."

"Balls." Hyde flapped her hands a few times to shoo Hamish away from her. "I should help."

"I think you should let the two of them sort it out." He sighed as they watched uncle and niece trudge up the embankment. "How about I give you a lift back to South Myrddin? It's on the way. You're technically a patient, and I think the Mini Cooper has driven its last lane. Not sure you're up for a walk."

"If I were an elder vampire, I could fade into shadow and appear wherever I want, defying the laws of physics." Hyde hadn't been graced with some of the abilities that often ran through vampire lines. "Maybe I'll take you up on your offer. Not sure I'm ready to wade into that conversation."

"Chief Inspector? I'll be giving Mx Snodgrass a lift back to the village. Just want to keep an eye on her for a few more minutes. Ms Pacheco? Would you care to join us? I'd like to make sure you're okay." Hamish, like most of the druids in the village, seemed to have a disdain for DCI Pacheco. Hyde had never been able to get to the bottom of it. It seemed to harken back to something having happened between Emrys and the vampire coven leader. "Did you need anything else?"

"A bottle of blood whiskey and a vacation," Pacheco muttered. "Get them out of here. I can ask them questions when they're not soaked to the bone."

The drive back to South Myrddin was far less cheerful. No music, for one. Hyde ignored the chatter between Rosa and Hamish. She stared blankly at a bit of mud on her fingers and allowed her mind to go blissfully blank.

Hamish dropped her off in front of the bookshop, admonishing her to call him or the doctor if she felt any aches or pains. "Try to keep out of trouble, will you?"

"I wasn't trying for this to happen. It just did." Hyde waved him off.

A sodden Hyde trudged towards the bookshop. She still had the emergency blanket wrapped around her. It glinted brightly in the sun and drew Teresa's attention.

"Hyde."

"Going inside now." Hyde's shoes squelched all the way up into her bedroom. She kicked them off and went immediately into the bathroom, stripping off all her ruined clothes. "I'm having a shower."

"Hyde?" Teresa called from outside the bathroom. "Are you okay?"

"I'm washing the loch off me."

"I… have questions."

"Give me a century to feel less like Nessie, and I'll tell you." Hyde tried in vain to rinse off the overall sensation of ick. "I do not enjoy being one with nature."

"I'll put out your comfy clothes."

After attempting to drown herself under the warm water until it ran cold, Hyde got changed and found Teresa down in the bookshop. They switched the sign from She to They. The day was a complete wash—literally and figuratively.

Teresa pressed a mug of calming tea into their hand and guided them to the armchairs by the fireplace. "Want to tell me what happened?"

"Something went wrong with Rosa's car, or something was in the lane. I'm not sure. We ended up launched into a loch." Hyde wrapped their hands around the mug, soaking in the warmth and leaning their head over to feel the steam on their face. "I don't think it would've killed us."

"Not sure that qualification makes it any less terrifying for you or the people who love you." Teresa sat on the edge of the armchair, leaning into Hyde. "How about I fix up one of my spiced soups? I've got some of the spicy blood sausages. You can stay all cosy here with the cats and a book while I whip up some lunch."

"Grimoire." Hyde cracked open one eye, then the other to glance around. "Might be upstairs."

"Will it strike me dead if I touch it?" Teresa smiled when Hyde rolled their eyes. "I'll grab it for you before I head out. Okay, Nessie?"

"Not Nessie. I washed the loch off me." Hyde sipped the tea, enjoying the stinging heat of it. "Loch Ness was named after a serpent shifter."

"It wasn't."

"It was. Emrys told me. Ness MacDougal. She had a tragic love affair with a warlock and disappeared a couple of centuries ago." Hyde balanced the mug on their knee. "It's true."

"Sounds like a gothic romance."

"Or tragedy."

16

TERESA

With Hyde safely ensconced with their cats and grimoire, Teresa rummaged through the records to find their favourite album by Away with the Faeries. The soft folk music was whimsical and gentle. It wouldn't intrude on their need for calm.

Leaving them alone in the shop, Teresa made sure the sign was turned to Closed and headed out to the taco bus. She'd work for another hour or two while putting a pot of soup on the stove to simmer. It would make for a hearty and warming late lunch.

The weather, while cold and grey, had turned into a dismal rain. Teresa had a decent flow of villagers popping in for a chat and tacos. She carefully deflected anyone who wandered too close to Between the Leaves. Thankfully, no one pushed the issue. Hyde definitely hadn't been up for visitors.

"Can I have two tacos, please?"

Teresa glanced up to see Gia Bassani in front of her. She tried to keep from visibly reacting to the beautiful blonde, not wanting to give anything away. "Of course. Anything else?"

"No." Gia shook her head. She glanced towards Between the Leaves after a few moments. "Is the bookshop not open today? I was hoping to find something to read since we're stuck here for a few more days while the police sort things out."

"Hyde took the day off. I'm sure it'll be open in the morning" Teresa kept her tone casual, which was an impressive feat given how her heart had started to race. "Are you not allowed to leave?"

"No. Quite obnoxious. I don't see what the point of us being here even is. They have Amalia in custody, I assume. What are we needed for?" Gia inspected her perfectly manicured nails. "We can't even put poor Rocco to rest. They have no respect for family rituals."

"I'm sure the police have their reasons." Teresa slowly put together the tacos. She wanted to draw the conversation out as long as possible. "Are your rituals similar to the Bassanis'?"

Gia's yellow eyes narrowed at the question. "Why would you ask?"

"Incubi and succubi usually have different rituals, as do families and covens."

"Ah. Yes." Gia still seemed suspicious but finally shook her head and relaxed again. "I'm not a succubus. They usually aren't compatible."

"Amalia and Battista are the obvious exceptions."

"Obviously," Gia sneered. "My family, the closest I could translate is that we are shadows. Shadow demons. Shades. The rest is closely guarded. Are the tacos ready? Honestly. How long does it take to slap them together?"

"Longer than you'd think." Teresa placed the tacos into a to-go box and handed it over. She accepted payment. "Why do you think Amalia would want Rocco dead?"

"Who knows? Perhaps she wanted to wrest control of the Bassani coven from him."

"Doesn't Enzo maintain control? He'd be the patriarch of the family." Teresa fixed up the second box and gave it to her. "And he seems capable of being the head."

Gia glanced around before leaning in closer. "There's a clause in the family bylaws. It allows the next in line to challenge for control of the coven and all assets connected to it when either the current head reaches a certain age or the heir does."

"And Rocco was of age?"

"He was. I should get these back to Enzo." Gia waved jauntily, then sauntered off as if she hadn't a care in the world.

There was something about the casual, almost disinterested way the woman talked about her deceased husband that bothered Teresa. Gia had not shown any signs of mourning Rocco. But what motivation could she possibly have for killing him?

She couldn't inherit it, not as someone who married into the family. It would be highly unlikely for her to be named next in line. It would go to Amalia and, if not to her, to another Bassani.

After working for another hour, Teresa closed up shop. The soup had simmered nicely. She finished cleaning up and then took a large container along with some fresh bread to the bookshop.

Thankfully, Mortar opened the door for her. Teresa made sure to shut and lock it before heading over to where Hyde was still ensconced in front of the fireplace in a mound of blankets. They didn't appear to have moved at all.

"I brought soup."

"Hmm?" Hyde blinked several times. It was a few seconds before they seemed able to focus, closing the grimoire and setting it off to the side. "Sorry. What?"

"Soup. And gossip. I have both in equal

measure." Teresa sat beside them. She poured the soup into two separate mugs, offering one to Hyde. "Gia Bassani came by for tacos."

"Did she?"

"She claims she's a shadow demon."

"Demon who can vanish in a wisp of smoke. Or maybe not disappear. It's almost like they wrap a cloak of darkness around themselves and blend into shadows." Hyde blew on the soup before taking a sip. "What is this?"

"My take on Mole de Olla. I used some of the left-over beef from the mole I made yesterday, along with potatoes and other vegetables, plus an extra blend of spices. It'll warm you right up." Teresa filled Hyde on how the rest of the conversation with Gia Bassani had gone. "If she can blend into the shadows, could she have made herself invisible at the restaurant? Enough to allow her to do whatever it is was done to the food?"

"I suppose." Hyde shrugged. They dug into the soup with relish, pointing their spoon at the grimoire. "I did some more reading. You'd think I'd reach the end of it at some point. There's always some other bit of information or another journal entry. The Snodgrasses were a pretentious bunch of vampires. I'm glad I was thrown aside. I couldn't imagine being so insufferable."

"That bad?"

"Worse." Hyde had another spoonful of soup. They wiped their mouth clean. "Did you use the moronga for this? I can always tell. The food is a little more satisfying. It sates both of my hungers."

"I did. I always keep a little on hand for you." Teresa knew a few of the other shifters and vampires who visited Guac-A-Mole enjoyed blood sausage as well. "Was there anything else interesting in your reading aside from pretentiousness?"

"There was. The smallest of passages about the Bassanis."

"Really? Why would your family have information on a demonic coven of incubi and succubi?" Teresa was honestly surprised Hyde was so open about sharing everything. Most coveted their grimoires jealously; they didn't seem to care. "Anything useful?"

"Maybe. Listen to this." Hyde set their mug down on the coffee table and grabbed the grimoire. They shifted down the sofa to sit beside Teresa, cracking open the large leather-bound book. "Vittoria Bassani claimed the title of coven leader through an insidious use of a peculiar family curse. The details are unknown, but it appears to be capable of turning a dish of food into a deadly concoction despite no actual poison being used."

"Well, that's not nothing."

"There are no other mentions of Vittoria, the Bassanis, or the curse, if it really was one." Hyde closed the grimoire and set it to the side once again. "Not exactly proof I can hand over to the police, but it definitely shows it's possible."

"Maybe we should ask Enzo about his ancestor Vittoria."

"Think he'd actually answer?" Hyde picked up their mug of soup and went back to eating. "I wouldn't if I were him."

"If he has nothing to hide, he might." Teresa slouched down on the sofa, pulling Mortar into her lap so she could rest against Hyde. "No harm in asking him."

"I mean, it's entirely possible that there might be harm in asking."

"I can't argue with that." Teresa chuckled. "We'll be extra careful."

17

HYDE

It was rare for Between the Leaves to be closed for an entire day. Hyde didn't often feel the need. They'd opened up late in the afternoon, not really expecting anyone.

The incident by the loch had thrown their entire day out of whack. Hyde tried to get back into reading the grimoire but failed. They finally returned it to the lockbox and began reorganising the shop.

One of their antique shelves was a little crooked. The side weaved in and out like waves. It made them look like something out of a fairy tale, which Hyde had always loved. They kept rare picture books and fantasy novels for the younger foundlings in the village—and some of the older ones as well.

Hyde picked up one of their personal favourites.

It was all about a vampire bunny that ran riot over a druid's garden. They'd always loved it when Emrys read the story to them as a wee fanged foundling. "Hello, old friend."

As Hyde flipped through the pages, the front door opened. A hiss from Mortar and then Pestle caught their attention. They were relatively calm cats who didn't bother the villagers who came into the shop—aside from Pacheco, occasionally.

They were surprised to find Enzo Bassani stepping inside the bookshop. It was hard to imagine him wanting to purchase something. He'd had plenty of time to do so previously.

"Mr Bassani. Can I help you?" Hyde set the book down and gathered up Mortar, who continued to hiss at the man. "Looking for a book?"

"I understand you have a talent for finding rare books; even ancient scrolls aren't beyond your reach." Enzo paid no mind to the angry cats, even when Pestle leapt onto the counter and kept a close eye on him. "Amalia was released."

Hyde frowned. They didn't understand how those two parts of the conversation were connected. "I'm glad they released her. They shouldn't have arrested her in the first place."

"Are you familiar with Veritas Verum?"

"Latin for 'true facts' or 'true words.' Something along those lines." Hyde clutched Mortar to their chest. The cat practically vibrated in their arms, hissing continually at Enzo. "It's also something the police can use to confirm someone's innocence, though most wouldn't dare submit to it."

In the area of the law, Veritas Verum referred to an ancient ritual that forced a person to divulge the absolute truth to questions. It had a controversial past and could no longer be required. There was a lengthy history of it being misused against innocent individuals to steal coven secrets.

"Correct. Amalia volunteered to undergo the ritual. Her attorney apparently ensured only questions connected to the murder and fire would be asked. She was cleared. Innocent." Enzo sneered at the last word.

Hyde kept space between them. Something about Enzo made them uneasy. They'd been around a variety of different demons; none had ever made her so uncomfortable. "Shouldn't you be pleased? I'd have thought you wouldn't want your daughter to be held for something she didn't do."

The look on his face was peculiar. Hyde didn't know how to decipher it. They wished Teresa was there to help.

"I understand you take commissions to hunt for rare manuscripts." Enzo sauntered over to one of the taller shelves. He ran a finger over one of the spines, making Hyde shudder. The scent of burnt feathers filled the air, though they couldn't identify why it bothered them so much. "Is that true?"

"I do." Hyde wanted nothing more than to drag the incubus away from their precious books. Mortar and Pestle continued to hiss lowly at him. "Why?"

"Our families have a shared history. A little thread connecting the Bassanis to the Snodgrasses." Enzo stopped inspecting a collection of fae sonnets and turned in their direction. "Important enough, I believe, for mentions in our respective grimoires. I believe you have yours. I'd be very interested in knowing what it says about us."

"Grimoires are private."

"They are." Enzo took a step towards them. He peered down when Pestle hissed at him. "Friendly cats."

"They're usually a good judge of character." Hyde moved back when he continued forward. Pestle continued to stay between her and Enzo. They struggled to keep a hold of Mortar. "Why are you here?"

"I want to see your grimoire."

"No." Hyde frowned at him. It was considered a massive invasion of privacy to demand anything regarding a family grimoire. They were closely guarded secrets. "I'd like you to leave."

Enzo pressed closer to them, eventually trapping them against the counter with no way to move past him. "I have to congratulate the druid. You'd have been burned alive without his intervention. Emrys has always been a formidable foe."

"You set the fire."

"It wouldn't have been my first choice. Fire isn't something I consider a speciality. I had help." Enzo shrugged indifferently, as if it didn't matter one way or the other to him. "I want your grimoire."

"Why? I can tell you there's very little about your family inside it." Hyde finally set Mortar on the counter to their right.

"I suppose I can satisfy your curiosity. I'm not being paid to return it to its rightful owner."

"Paid?" Hyde had heard all the words, but they struggled to comprehend what he was saying.

"Nothing so plebeian as money exchanged hands." Enzo continued to inch closer to them, completely disregarding the cats in his path. "A debt was owed to someone in your family—and I intend to repay it."

"By what? By whom?"

"Making you disappear and returning the Snod-grass grimoire into the right hands."

"I don't understand. What does any of this have to do with Rocco? Was his death an accident? Was I the target?" Hyde prepared themselves for a fight. They considered their options carefully, trying to figure out if they could safely make it to one of the exits. "I thought I was collateral damage."

"Oh, no. You are just a little detour." Enzo was infuriatingly blasé about his deadly intent. "The intention of coming to your quaint village was always for my son to die."

"Why? Why would you do that?"

"I refuse to lose control over my family. Upstart punk thought he could reconcile with his sister. They would take the Bassanis into the future." Enzo clenched his fists at his side. He slammed one against the counter, causing Hyde and the cats to flinch. "Rocco is no longer a concern. My plans for Amalia didn't quite work out, but no matter. She'll be dealt with eventually."

Hyde was too far away to trigger the emergency alarm Emrys had built into the shop. They thought they might be able to make it to the back door. They needed to keep Enzo talking and distracted. "Who called in a family debt?"

"Magnus."

Hyde was genuinely stunned by the response.

"Magnus? Why would my uncle, who I haven't seen in decades, want me dead?"

"I neither know nor care." Enzo reached into his jacket pocket and pulled out a long, curved dagger. "It's been years since I spilt vampire blood."

"*Balls.*"

18

TERESA

Teresa had been doing some prep for the next morning when a scream followed by glass breaking interrupted the quiet evening. "What the—"

Rushing out of the bus, she stumbled to a halt. Enzo Bassani appeared to have gone crashing through the front windows of Between the Leaves. He lay prone on the ground in the middle of the glass and broken wood.

"You threw my cat." Hyde stormed out of the bookshop. They leapt at Enzo, who'd been trying to pull himself out of the glass. Teresa cleared her throat a couple of times. "I will… oh. Resa. Hello."

"Hello." Teresa suppressed a highly inappropriate urge to laugh. "Shall I call the police?"

"Would you?" Hyde casually restrained Enzo as if it were nothing at all. "I lost my temper."

In the years Teresa had known Hyde, she'd never seen them "lose their temper." If it were going to happen, attacking the cats was definitely a way to do it. Teresa quickly sent a text to Emrys and then called the police.

"Release me." Enzo tried to throw Hyde off.

"Shan't."

"Hyde? Are Mortar and Pestle okay?"

Hyde had their elbow pressing Enzo to the ground, showing an impressive use of their strength. Something they almost never did. It was easy to forget they were a vampire from an ancient line. "They're fine. I told them to stay inside to avoid the glass."

"Get off me."

"No. And quit wasting your energy. You're making my skin itch. Vampires aren't affected by your powers. Didn't my uncle tell you?" Hyde knocked him back against the pavement. "You should've left my cats alone."

To Teresa's relief, Constable Antonov showed up relatively quickly. With help from Santi, who'd come rushing out of his craft shop, they managed to secure handcuffs on Enzo. Teresa assumed they were the demonic-specific ones to dampen his abilities. Enzo was shoved into the back of the police car while Teresa helped Hyde stand up.

"I sent Aadil a text message about your broken windows. He'll be here to board them up for you this evening and come back in the morning to start working on replacing them." Rosa gave Hyde a reassuring smile. "Were you hurt?"

"Hyde?" Teresa was worried when they didn't answer.

Instead of responding, Hyde raced back into the shop. Teresa followed behind them. It wasn't a surprise when they went to round up their cats, making sure they were okay.

"Hyde? Did he hurt you?" Teresa repeated her question. Her heart started to race at the idea of some hidden injury. She couldn't stop mentally listing all the possibilities, from a scratch to a hit artery. "Hyde?"

"Hmm?"

"Are you okay?" Teresa had to clear her throat a few times to get the question out.

"I'm fine."

"I am not panicking. I'm not. Nothing to panic about now. Everything is fine." Teresa paced by the bookshop counter, taking quick and shallow breaths. "Everything is fine."

Hyde twisted back around towards her. They seemed to finally notice the state of her, coming over to take her hands. "Resa? I did far more damage to him than he did to me. I don't have a scratch on me. My hands are a little sore from hitting him."

"You're okay."

"I am okay." Hyde sounded as unsure as Teresa felt.

"Maybe if we say the words a hundred more times, we'll believe them." Teresa guided Hyde over to the couch. They both sank down on it. "Why don't you take a few deep breaths?"

"I think we should both breathe and flail mentally together for a moment." Hyde dropped their head forward between their legs. "Can vampires pass out?"

"I've seen you do it." Teresa rubbed her hand lightly over Hyde's back. The motion was soothing for both of them. She tried to pay attention to the things around her. The orange of Pestle's fur, the sounds from outside, the glowing light from the fireplace. All her senses were engaged in the effort to pull back from a panic attack. "How about we both take a few deep breaths?"

"Excellent plan. Wonderful plan. Brilliant, even. What is breathing?" Hyde laughed a little hysterically. They finally sat up after several minutes. "I never liked those windows."

Teresa tilted her head to rest against Hyde's briefly. They both glanced towards the door when it opened. Pacheco strode in with Emrys close behind. "I sense questions are going to be asked."

"And we thought Fynn was the seer." Hyde tensed when Pacheco moved around to stand in front of them. He seemed to notice and took a few steps back, going to sit in a nearby armchair.

"Can you tell me what happened?" Pacheco got straight to the point.

"He said he wanted my grimoire. My uncle sent him to get rid of me and steal it back. A *side* jaunt after killing his own son and framing Amalia." Hyde bent over to lift Mortar and Pestle into their arms. They set them both on the couch and ran their fingers through the cats' fur. "He had a knife. I think it went under one of the armchairs. I lost sight of it."

"You lost sight of it?"

"He lunged at me. Mortar leapt onto his face. He tossed her aside and kicked Pestle." Hyde ran their fingers over the latter. "He's okay, I think. I threw Enzo through the windows."

"You threw him through the windows?"

"He attacked my furry friends." Hyde cuddled the cats closer, glowering at Pacheco. "I might not make a show of what I can do, but I will protect Mortar and Pestle with my life."

"Why did he want your grimoire?" Emrys asked before Pacheco could.

"My uncle did." Hyde shrugged. "He apparently wanted me dead as well."

Teresa broke the stunned silence when she could see both Pacheco and Emrys struggling to contain their rage. They were both aware that Hyde didn't do well with raw emotions like anger. "But why go to all of this after ignoring you for decades? And why set the place on fire?"

"The grimoire wouldn't burn even in sacred fire. It's almost indestructible." Hyde dragged their fingers roughly through their ginger curls. "Maybe he thought he could sneak in once the fire had ravaged the shop and grab it without anyone noticing?"

"We're taking him into interrogation. I *will* be asking him about your uncle." Pacheco stood back up. He was so tense that his face seemed carved out of stone. "I'll take care of your family."

Hyde seemed as stunned by the ferocity of Pacheco's statement as Teresa. They watched him stalk out of the shop before turning towards Emrys. "What was that?"

"Jonatan Pacheco remembering who he used to be." Emrys smiled somewhat bitterly. He moved over to sit on the coffee table in front of Hyde. "Were you hurt? Should I give Hamish or Wilfred a call? Have them check you out?"

"I'm fine. Shaky but uninjured." Hyde threw their arm out towards the gaping hole in the front of the shop. "Better than my poor baby."

"Windows and walls can be easily repaired. You can't." Emrys patted them gently on the arm, then moved to sit in one of the armchairs to give them more space. "We'll get them boarded up for now—and maybe Aadil can work his magic with glass and create another beautiful masterpiece."

"My uncle."

"Leave your family to me… and Pacheco." Emrys added the latter after a moment of thought. "We'll handle the problem."

Hyde watched Emrys leave in silence before turning to Teresa. "Is it just me, or was that odd?"

"The Pacheco part? Decidedly odd." Teresa tried to tune out the noise that was still coming from outside. "They hate each other."

"They do."

"Have they always hated each other?" Teresa hadn't known either Pacheco or Emrys as long as Hyde.

"I have no idea. For as long as I've known them, at least."

19

HYDE

It had been almost two in the morning before Hyde had even attempted to get sleep. They kept waking up, imagining Enzo or their uncle had snuck into the shop. Teresa stayed over. Her presence and the cats draped haphazardly across their body helped them calm down after each nightmare.

They managed to extract themselves from the cats and Teresa's arms. Their mind whirled around like an out-of-control Ferris wheel. It made staying asleep nigh impossible.

A muffled banging caught their attention as they stared into their wardrobe. Hyde quickly threw on clean clothes and tried to exit the upstairs flat without waking Teresa. They rushed downstairs only to breathe a sigh of relief when they spotted Aadil.

Aadil Fadel was djinn of all trades. He ran the

local garage and was a talented glazier who specialised in stained-glass windows. They often signed about ancient Egyptian scrolls together when he wasn't amusing himself by teaching Mortar and Pestle BSL, or British Sign Language; the cats picked it up far more quickly than Hyde had.

Thankfully for both of them, Aadil read lips better than Hyde signed. It wasn't always a guarantee of understanding, but they managed.

Hyde stepped outside, drawing their cardigan tightly around them in the crisp morning air. They waved when Aadil spotted them, signing and speaking their hello. "You're up early."

"I'm taking measurements and ensuring the plywood is secure enough to last the few weeks it's going to take me to do another stained-glass masterpiece," Aadil signed. He finished getting his last measurement before turning back towards them. "Are you okay?"

"Mostly."

"Sure?" Aadil waited until she'd nodded to continue. "The windows are all boarded up. Not the most beautiful of sights, but I'll have your new ones ready in about three weeks."

"Thank you." Hyde gave him a quick hug. They knew he would refuse to take any sort of payment from them. "I could—"

"Find a lovely book for me to read?" Aadil cut them off with a sharp wave before they could even offer payment. "Excellent. I'll pop by tomorrow with a few design ideas for your windows."

Signing their goodbyes, Hyde watched Aadil drive off in his van. They sighed when a familiar unmarked police vehicle pulled into the space the djinn had vacated. DCI Pacheco looked as if he hadn't slept at all in the past twenty-four hours.

"Morning." Hyde still wasn't sure what to think of his reaction the previous night. There were layers of the brief conversation they'd definitely missed. "Something wrong?"

"I thought you might want to know Enzo Bassani made a full confession early this morning. He intended all along to kill his son and frame his daughter. Your uncle provided information on the blood ritual required to poison the dish in exchange for killing you and retrieving the grimoire." Pacheco didn't sugar-coat anything. "The ashes you found at the shore were the remnants of a ritual to keep Gia Bassani from warning you or speaking to the police. He quite literally bound her tongue."

"Why would my uncle do this? I haven't spoken to anyone in my family since I was abandoned." Hyde had gone out of their way to avoid mentioning them until the grimoire arrived just recently. "I don't understand."

"Enzo claims he has no idea what the motivation was aside from wanting the grimoire returned." Pacheco was even more serious than usual. He patted them awkwardly on the shoulder, as if trying to offer comfort. "I've called a meeting in the coven demanding the heads of the families attend. I won't let this continue."

Hyde could only shrug. They'd never seen Pacheco do anything to reel in the vampire families under his leadership. "Okay."

They stood silently for several seconds. Hyde's attention was drawn by someone walking in the distance. They frowned, trying to determine why the man seemed so familiar.

"What the dickens? Bram?" Hyde dodged around Pacheco. They raced down the pavement, following the tall man with the guitar slung on his back. "Bram!"

The man stopped walking. He turned slowly and broke into a wide grin. His wavy brown hair was shoulder length and wildly uncontrolled, partially blocking his stormy blue eyes.

"Mo chridhe."

"I'm not your heart. Don't be weird." Hyde braced themselves for the strong embrace. He didn't disappoint, stalking forward, throwing his arms around them, and lifting them off their feet to swing them around. "What brings you back to the village?"

"Heard a few rumours on the wind and found myself swept back this way." Bram released them. He rested his hands on their shoulders while he got a good look at them. "My feet always find a way of leading me home to my family, mo chridhe."

Hyde had missed him despite his eccentricities. "I have a book for you."

"Oh?"

"All about the Loch Ness myth. Been saving it for over fifteen years. You've been gone a long while. I've missed you."

"The winds carried me away. The court required my attention, but now they've carried me back." Bram looped his arm around their shoulders. "Now, tell me about this bus outside your shop and the beautiful witch I see standing near it. She's had an eye on me since you came rushing over to me. Did you finally give your heart to someone?"

"Bram." Hyde peered back to find Teresa had come out of the bookshop. They hadn't seen her in their rush to meet him. "Teresa. She's a witch and runs a taco bus."

"And?"

"She's my girlfriend," Hyde admitted.

"Then she has good taste." Bram set one of his bags down. "My home in the lighthouse is all shut up. I'll be cleaning things out, but we'll catch up. You can tell me why your shop is all boarded up."

"I threw someone through it."

"I'm going to need a few more details filled in." Bram ruffled their red curls, grinning when they batted his hand away. "I have missed you, little vampire."

Bram was Bram. Hyde had no idea how to describe him to anyone who hadn't met him before. He was almost as much of a legend as Emrys.

No one knew when Bram had arrived in South Myrddin. He was as wild and untamed as his wavy brown hair. A roaming busker whom Emrys had once described as a semi-feral member of the Seelie Court. The music he created tended to be dark yet ethereal; it carried the listener away to magical and dangerous places.

"Does Emrys know you've returned?" Hyde chose to ignore his myriad of pet names.

"He does." Emrys came around the corner to join them. He glowered at Bram. "It's an odd coincidence that you've returned just as someone's been causing mischief in the village."

"Is it?"

"It was you, wasn't it? Behind all those cursed

letters? Just the sort of inane nonsense you would pull." Emrys glowered at Bram, who merely shrugged in response. "Typical. Never caring about the chaos you leave behind in your wake. Never bothered about anyone but yourself."

"I caused no harm, just a bit of fun." Bram shrugged.

"Emrys." Hyde stepped between the two. They didn't want things to devolve immediately when Bram had just returned. "I'm sure he's sorry."

"I'm sure he's not." Emrys managed a smile for Hyde. "I'll come by the bookshop later."

"As will I."

Hyde didn't get another word in edgewise as the druid and fae stalked away from each other. *Balls.*

They'd hoped to ask if Emrys planned to attend the "we're not being arrested" party at Al Dente. Battista had promised to make Teresa's favourite stew. Hyde hoped this time they'd all get to enjoy it and none of the dishes would be poisoned.

"What was that all about?" Teresa walked over to where Hyde stood, still watching Bram and Emrys stalk away in opposite directions. "Bad blood?"

"Bad something. They've never been close, but I've never seen them quite this prickly with each other." Hyde was surprised at the ferocity of Emrys's disapproval. That was usually reserved for Pacheco.

They shivered when a cold breeze swept up off the loch. "I have a dreadful feeling this Yule isn't going to be quite so blessed."

"It'll be fine." Teresa looped her arms around Hyde, drawing them into a kiss. They both ignored the whistles from a few villagers passing by. "I'm sure it'll all be fine."

Hyde returned the kiss before stepping back. They caught one last glimpse of Bram before he disappeared around a corner. "Whatever happens, we'll manage it together. Somehow."

BE SURE TO CHECK OUT FOR BOOK THREE, A MERRY MURDEROUS MIDWINTER.

ACKNOWLEDGMENTS

A massive thank-you to my brilliant betas and the crew in my Cozies by the Fire group who helped brainstorm some of the names in the book. To Becky, Kristin, and all the fantastic people at Tangled Tree and Hot Tree Publishing. And also to my beloved hubby, who keeps me from losing my mind while I'm stressing over word counts.

And, lastly, thank you, readers, for following me on my writing journey. I hope you enjoyed *A Fatal Autumnal Stew* and are looking forward to book three.

ABOUT THE AUTHOR

Dahlia Donovan wrote her first romance series after a crazy dream about shifters and damsels in distress. She prefers irreverent humour and unconventional characters. An autistic and occasional hermit, her life wouldn't be complete without her husband and her massive collection of books and video games.

Don't miss out on new releases, exclusive give-aways, and much more!

JOIN DAHLIA'S NEWSLETTER:

HTTP://EEPURL.COM/Q0N0X

JOIN HER READER GROUP:

WWW.FACEBOOK.COM/GROUPS/1108750876162947

SHE'D LOVE TO HEAR FROM YOU DIRECTLY, TOO. PLEASE FEEL FREE TO EMAIL HER AT DAHLIA@DAHLIADONOVAN.COM OR CHECK OUT HER WEBSITE HTTPS://DAHLIADONOVAN.COM/ FOR UPDATES.

facebook.com/dahliadonovan

x.com/DahliaDonovan

instagram.com/dahliadonovanauthor

pinterest.com/dahliadonovan

ABOUT THE PUBLISHER

Hot Tree Publishing loves love. Publishing adult romantic fiction, HTPubs are all about diverse reads featuring heroes and heroines to swoon over. Since opening in 2015, HTPubs have published more than 300 titles across the wide and diverse range of romantic genres. If you're chasing a happily ever after in your favourite subgenre, HTPubs have you covered.

Interested in discovering more amazing reads brought to you by Hot Tree Publishing? Head over to the website for information:

WWW.HOTTREEPUBLISHING.COM

facebook.com/hottreepublishing

x.com/hottreepubs

instagram.com/hottreepublishing

tiktok.com/@hottreepublishing

www.ingramcontent.com/pod-product-compliance
Lightning Source LLC
Chambersburg PA
CBHW061445210726
48287CB00007B/2371